RESURGENT

T. L. Riffey

Publishing Coordinator – Sharon Kizziah-Holmes

Paperback-Press
an imprint of A & S Publishing
A & S Holmes, Inc.

ISBN -13: 978-1-951772-31-4

DEDICATION

Dedicated to those who took a chance and read this book.

ACKNOWLEDGMENTS

Thanks to those who encouraged me to start writing again.

ONE

Strader Ruins
Greenpeace
1270 Standard

The inside of Sara's mouth tasted as though it had been soaked in a mixture of brine and fuel. Her forearm throbbed, bringing her back to reality, and she pulled herself out of the cot to stand on unsteady legs. Wind whipped the tent as intently as the rain, making it seem to her as if the weather conspired to keep her within the camp, within the cliff wall's domain.

There hadn't been a cloud in the dawning sky when Sara had awaken to find herself being carried into the camp, having—fortunately—missed being lowered to the ground in a hastily rigged stretcher.

She had been given Terran whiskey to drink as the Camp's only medic—the Professor's assistant, a woman called Bet—had bandaged her arm after a session with a knitter and had her taken to a cot with orders to sleep. How long ago that had been she wasn't sure as she had vague memories of being fed and re-bandaged twice.

Her eyes sharpened as the tent flap was thrown back and a form entered the tent. The man shoved a lock of ash-blond hair off his brow as he threw his hat onto one of the other cots and turned his dark eyes toward her. "I see you're feeling better," he said as he slipped the poncho over his head and threw it to join his hat on the cot.

"And you are?"

"Foster."

She noted the guarded look in his eyes and smiled grimly. "As you probably already know, I'm Sara Connor."

"The Ghost of the Ruins," Foster commented.

"Where's the Professor?"

"With the others up in the chamber." He sat on his cot with a tired sigh and rubbed his eyes. His body appeared relaxed, but that didn't fool her for one minute. "You sure did cause a royal ruckus," he told her with a boyish smile. "The Professor was practically in Heaven when she saw that Chamber."

Sara recalled the short, petite blond in green coveralls with gentle brown eyes as she hovered behind her brunette assistant anxiously. "I'm glad I made someone's day."

Foster chuckled as he buried his head in his hands. "That you did. The Professor gave the lieutenant a browbeating that would have done credit to a General."

"Another friendship down the tubes," she sighed as she fell onto her cot. Her body was leaden as though her blood had been replaced with mercury.

Nearly choking on laughter, Foster raised his head and looked at her. "You're not at all what I expected…"

"So say they all." She grimaced as she remembered the others that had come to the ruins. They too couldn't believe she was the Madwoman or the Ghost of the Ruins as some of the natives called her. "The priests and the Port's Guards paint a false picture with their misunderstandings."

Her head lowered as her eyes closed and she felt his stare, yet didn't raise her head. "Why do they hate you so?" she heard him ask almost inaudible and with a sigh she raised her head. Meeting his eyes, she noted his startled look, but didn't realize how different she looked to him with that serious cast to her face.

"You saw what I did up there?" At his nod, she dropped her eyes. "I have had to do that before…Though usually with rogue off-worlders not Guests."

Foster frowned and she could almost sense the multitude of thoughts that flickered behind his eyes. But she could guess the main question and answered it with a half-truth.

"The natives are of the Sect Degar, which is an off-shoot of the Religion of Elgar."

"Elgar…" he broke off as if he didn't know how to phrase the question. "I don't understand."

"It is believed to be an extinct religion. The man I stabbed made himself a sacrifice, a sacrifice to bring the wrath of the Death God—and the Degar Priests upon this dig as well as upon me." His face tightened as she saw the meaning of her words dawn on him. "Though the act of me killing them would have already done that."

"Then we can expect them to show up sometime soon."

Professor Maher with the lieutenant at her heels had entered the tent while Sara had been talking, yet she had not heard or sensed them which made her angry—at herself. She had let down her guard and had she been elsewhere she would have been dead.

"Then we can expect them?" The Professor repeated the lieutenant's words, but making them a question this time.

"The off-worlder priests don't like to be denied. But it is the native priests that will come for the reckoning as those I killed had Guest-rights."

"Yet you have denied them," Foster commented. "You obviously stopped them before they could do whatever they had planned."

Her head lowered as her strength gave out. Yes, she could deny them, but the reason was not what they suspected. She was not one of them, nor was she somehow immune to their weapons as the slashes on her arm showed. Death had little hold over her as it did not threaten her. IT had been her companion since the day she was born, since the day her people...

A hand lifted her head and a cup was pressed against her lips. Sipping, she looked into Foster's face and knew he understood. "I'm alright, desert-born," she muttered as he took the cup away.

"You need rest," he stated with a glare at the cup in his hand.

Sara smiled faintly, "My people do not run from death, nor do we forget duty…"

"I should have guessed," growled the lieutenant as he backed a step in disgust. "That coppery hair…"

"Many spacers have copper hair, Lieutenant" The Professor met Sara's eyes. "That does not mean they are all Ilan."

"Besides, the Ilan genocided over seven decades ago, you know that, Lieutenant" Foster added his voice to the Professor's argument. "Though it appears their religion continues."

The lieutenant regained his self-control as his mind grasped this last statement. "This religion, what exactly is it about?"

It was the Professor who answered him, not Sara. " Kali, a deity of Death was worshiped by many of the colonist who first settled many of the harsher worlds during the Rim years. Originally the god was female, but over the centuries it change with many of the planets, changing the name as well as the sex. Degar, the Demi-god of this planet's natives is one example. Once there was space travel again, the Death Cult sprang up, joining many of the death religions together."

"The Ilan religion of Elgar was the largest group in the Death Cult at that time, encompassing three systems." Sara's eyes swept over their faces. "The Death Cult reined supreme in many Systems until the Federation returned their attentions to the colonial planets after their War. The United Church is what brought on the Genocide of the Ilan…"

"What?" The others looked at her as if she was insane.

Her eyes were unfocused as though she looked into the far past. "A missionary told us—the Ilan-- of Jesis, the Forgiving Child. Many of my—the Ilan flocked to hear of this child who died to save all people from the displeasure of his Father. The Priests did not like this, of course."

"I'll bet," muttered Foster.

"What followed was an Illena, or a holy war as you would call it. Followers of both sides trained warriors…warriors that often traded sides."

"And which were you?"

"My sister," she continued as though the lieutenant had not spoken. "was a PSI healer—and a follower of Jesis. Father thought it best that I be trained by the Elgar priest…"

"A foot in both camps," commented Foster.

"Perhaps so; I do not know. The Priests taught me well, too well, I now think. But they made a mistake in believing I would turn on my own sister…The Priest should not have told me to hurt her." This last was said in an almost childish voice full of resentment.

"What happen?" the Professor asked softly.

Sara's eyes met the Professor's. "I killed the Corin, The High Priest. The so-called Prophet. "

"That happened over 70 years ago!"

"Seventy-two years ago actually."

Foster studied her briefly. "You are not over

twenty-five Standards."

"I'm almost a hundred Standard years old," she told him with a slanted look. "I fled with my sister to the Port where we stowed away on a freighter bound for the next system. We both signed on to work on another ship heading for the inner systems. It never made it…"

"The *Bran*," murmured the Professor.

"Yes," she told the Professor, her mouth in a straight grim line. Pain lanced through her at the memory, and she dropped her head. "I do not wish to recall that time."

"Ilan…"

Sara raised her head and met the lieutenant's eyes, unaware of the reckless gleam that made her eyes glitter like a cat's. "I am Lendri. The Ilan are dead."

"When should we expect these Priests?"

As if in answer to the lieutenant's question, an explosion shook the ground. A voice called out in the native language and was answered by stunner-fire, even as the lieutenant vanished out the tent flap. He returned moments later, holding a black arrow in his hand.

"It is an Athian," Sara answered his unspoken question. "A declaration of war, if you will. It shows intent to challenge."

"War against us or against you?"

"That symbol etched on the arrowhead says me, though they will kill you to get to me, to make me suffer their pain."

"Their pain?"

"They prefer mental pain above all tortures, and I

did the worse kind of wrong to one of the Clan. I killed his Guests. I am now the Priests' meat."

"Meat?"

"The object of their hunting," she clarified with a shrug. "Part of their justice system is allowing opponents the opportunity to strenuously object with sharp objects."

"That seems barbaric." The lieutenant was frowning.

"The Clans can be barbaric. Their level of technology is about what Terra was in the nineteenth century with a little twentieth thrown in but their society is Terra's Irish Clans of the sixteenth and seventeenth century."

"That's about right," the professor said.

"If the Priests are going to come here soon to formally challenge you, you need to rest." Foster pointed to a cot.

Sara obediently lay down.

Foster looked at the professor and the lieutenant and pointed to the tent flap.

"She doesn't seem too concerned about these Priests," the lieutenant observed to the Professor as the tent flap slid shut behind them.

The Professor hunched her shoulders against the wind-driven rain as they moved toward the Mess tent, her face thoughtful. "I believe it's more acceptance or resignation than unconcern. As she has said, her people never ran from Death; they accepted things as they came."

"No use worrying about something until it happens, ay?"

"Something like that...This Hunting is what

worries me. With her injury, she won't be able to maintain for whatever the period of the hunt may be before she can challenge the Priests' rulings."

"I still don't understand that Hunting stuff. Why don't they just kill her outright and be done with it instead of this-chasing-her-and-wounding-her-if-caught, then-letting her-go-again crap."

"All part of the torture, Lieutenant. Wear her down mentally as well as physically before killing her. If the person can survive the Hunt without food or rest, then the Priests will hear a challenge to the reason the person was being Hunted. They believe if the person lives that long they are blessed by Degar."

"What good if the Hunted dies in the challenge?"

"Well, the Hunted doesn't *have* to fight; another could stand in that person's stead if someone is on the Hunted's side. But with that injury, she's already wore down…"

"I'm thinking she'll be the one standing by the end of this Hunt," the lieutenant said as he swept open the mess tent's door. "I think the Priests have met their match."

Two

Two stick knives and a handful of darts lay in a half circle before Sara, each getting an individual inspection. The professor had returned her stick knife so she at least had it again. Fingers lingered over the edges carefully testing the sharpness, sliding down the handles to ensure wholeness. She would have to make more darts if the Hunt lasted long, though when she would be able to she didn't know.

Her special abilities should give her an edge, but the knives and darts were like a security blanket, safe and comfortable. She knew she may have to do permanent damage to the natives that would be hunting her. This would be the first hunt that she was the hunted but she had witnessed two hunts since she had come here. Each had barely lasted a day. She wanted to last much longer.

Like the entire time.

The Laren had prepared her well for hit-and-run missions. Perhaps she should use the same tactics here. The Priests wouldn't be expecting that, and the off-worlders wouldn't be prepared for it. It would at least keep them busy with their own concerns, until the deadline hopefully.

With a flick of her wrist, a blade of energy appeared in her hand. In shape it resembled a shuriken of ancient Terra, and was thrown as such. The jolt it gave caused a brief paralysis so a shot to the heart or throat could kill, but otherwise it just caused immobility. Several hits could cause unconsciousness as well. It was one of the standard bio-mechanicals that the Laren had given her that couldn't be taken away like the knives and darts before her.

The Laren. Finding the hidden cavern was a shock. It reminded her of the underground laboratory where they had taken her and Litty when the Laren had changed them. Was this another of their installations that they had built during their War with the Cren or was it built at another time? If only she had time to explore.

Another flick of her wrist and the energy blade disappeared. Testing anything else would have to wait and be done in the field anyway. Staying awake the whole time of the hunt and still being able to fight the Priests' champion might be a problem. After all she was still human, no matter what the Laren had done to her.

She gathered up the knives and darts and returned them to their places before standing.

The professor entered the tent with the High Priest and Rolad, the lieutenant bringing up the rear. Foster slid in and stood beside Sara.

Sara spit on the ground before Rolad. "Brother-killer."

Rolad merely raised an eyebrow.

"Your petition will be heard second moon rise three days from now," the Priest said. "Rolad will be the champion."

She inclined her head.

"Five are your pursuers." the Priest continued.

Sara glanced at Rolad and seeing his smirk, knew some of his off-world 'friends' would be hunting her as well. After all his father had guested seven off-worlders and she'd only accounted for four. And who knew what was up the off-worlders' proverbial sleeves.

"The Hunt shall begin at second moon rise." The Priest paused as he glanced at the Terrans. "Any who interfere do so at their own risk."

"I shall be gone from here by then," Sara told the Priest. "I would not endanger the Accords between the Clans and the Terrans."

"Good." The Priest inclined his head. "Until the time of the petition."

"Until then," she said.

Roland and the Priest left the tent with Foster trailing behind them to ensure they left camp.

"How did they come up with this cockamamie way of doing things?" the lieutenant exclaimed as soon as they were sure the natives were out of hearing range.

"It's a mixture of Terran and Ilan. Trial by

combat mixed with a trial of worthiness."

"Seems stacked in the Priests' favor," the Professor said.

"Of course." Sara gave a bit of a laugh, though there was no humor in it. "How else do you think they've stayed in power. And of course, the Federation has that non-interference rule toward local planetary governments and their people."

"That doesn't apply towards you," the lieutenant Said. "You could make a case that those men were interfering in local matters."

"But that won't change the local laws." She waved her hand. "The natives, especially the Priests, need to realize what is happening. The Elgar Death Cult must not get a foothold here or they will have a base from which to spread further. We do not want another Ilan."

"No. Which is why I sent a message to Command," the lieutenant said. "The ship they arrived in is being watched and they are restricted to the Port for now."

"My disposition will be dependent upon whether I survive," Sara told him.

"You told us enough." the lieutenant waved his hand. "And the rest speaks for itself."

"Can you tell us anything about the chamber?" Professor Maher asked. "And why there are tunnels that lead to dead ends."

"I'm thinking those dead ends are anything but. There's probably a mechanism that opens them up. As to the chamber, the man obviously thought the basin was a sacrificial pool. Did you speak with the survivor?"

"He just starts chanting when you ask him anything."

"Have you spoken with the Priests about it?" Sara asked.

The Lt and the professor exchanged looks, then the Professor said, "No. We thought it best to wait."

"Probably a good idea," Sara said. "They won't hear anything bad about guests of the brother of their High Priest. And the High Priest may pressure to cancel your VISA or at the very least tell the native diggers not to dig for you anymore."

"That crossed our minds," the professor told her. "So you don't have any ideas about that chamber?"

Sara shrugged. She knew what the chamber was. Or at least she suspected what the whole place was. An outpost of the Laren. However, she wasn't going to explain how she knew that. They already knew more about her than she was comfortable with. "Laren, obviously from the graphs, but from there your guess is as good as mine."

The professor stared at her for a moment, then nodded, "Alright."

"They're away," Foster told them, returning just then. "I don't like that younger native. He smells wrong."

"He's in with the off-worlders." Sara made a gesture toward the cliff. "You probably smell a mix of their scents on him"

"I did smell them but something else smells wrong about him." Foster paused. "And his eyes were bloodshot. Could he have been high on something?"

Sara inhaled sharply as something occurred to

her.

Foster looked at her and raised an eyebrow.

"There used to be an Ilan drug that acted like a stimulant and an aphrodisiac. It's highly addictive. Those men had Ilan poison so they might have had that drug too."

"Our scanners registered the substance as poison on those claws, but you're saying it's Ilan." The lieutenant stated more than asked.

"Yes." Sara nodded. "The poison eats your body away with a mixture of pain and pleasure, driving you mad before shutting your organs down. How fast it works depends on how hydrated you are. Now the stimulant keeps you in a state of pleasure while depleting your body of nutrients and liquid to ensure your awareness."

"Water seems to be a reoccurring theme," Foster said.

"It's sacred. Elgar came from the water and returned to the water." Sara shrugged. "That is what we were told anyway."

"Baptism," Foster murmured.

Sara nodded.

"What?" the lieutenant asked.

"How the Church got a toe-hold in. I imagine that they had a public baptism pool."

Sara nodded again.

The professor's mouth went round in realization.

His eyes went to the professor then to Foster before a flicker of realization lit them. "Oh," the lieutenant said then.

A grim smile touched Sara's lips. "Oh, indeed."

Bet, the professor's assistant, appeared behind

the Professor and handed her a tablet. "Everything's getting cataloged and snapped as ordered," she told the professor before moving to Sara. "How's the arm? You didn't tear anything, did you?"

Sara turned her arm to show Bet the still sealed knife wound. The knitter had sterilized and sealed the wound and Sara had been careful not to use it a lot. It took at least forty-eight hours for a knitted wound to be healed enough that any use wouldn't reopen the wound.

"Excellent if I do say so myself," Bet said with a smile.

"Thank you."

Bet nodded then turned back to the professor. "I'm going back and keep an eye on the boys."

The professor gestured her agreement with her free hand, her eyes on the tablet.

With a shake of her head, Bet left, and Sara looked toward the tablet.

"Those pics of the chamber?"

"And the cave," the professor said, not looking up.

"I'd advise you to get what you can," Sara said. "The High Priest may want you gone when this is over, for one reason or another. So your Visa may be revoked even though you have nothing to do with this fight."

"Do you think they'll harass us while they're hunting you?" the lieutenant asked, even as the professor opened her mouth.

"Not overly, but there are some who don't like off-worlders period so they may take this time to show their displeasure."

"I'll keep up the extra measures then." The lieutenant paused. "Anything we should know security wise?"

"Don't trust any of the priests or those close to them. Some are devoted and honorable by their lights but most are greedy and care only for their position. Most of your diggers and helpers are common folk so you shouldn't have too much trouble with them but the priests may stir them up for their own agendas. It would be best not to let Bet or the professor be alone among them."

The lieutenant nodded acknowledgement.

"Now surely," the professor began to protest.

"Not up for debate," the lieutenant said before she could say more. "It's part of the reason I'm here."

"You're here because of protocol," the professor said. "Not because of any real threat."

"Well, it's real now," the lieutenant told her.

Foster shoved a backpack into Sara's chest, her arms going around it automatically. "Here. Just a bit for the Hunt."

"Thank you."

The lieutenant and the professor walked away with a wave still arguing.

"What's with those two? You'd think they were married or at least dating."

"Oh, the tension, you mean?" Foster glanced toward the direction the other two went then looked at Sara. "It's not sexual no matter how it looks. They really do get on each other's nerves."

"Huh." Sara shook her head to get her thoughts organized. The professor and her crew were really none of her business except in a general way. However, Greenpeace and its people were. "I need to get some sleep before I leave. Thanks for the backpack."

By the smile on Foster's face, Sara knew he got the dismissal, and she watched as he left her alone. She would look through the backpack after she slept. This would likely be the only real sleep she would get in the next three days.

THREE

The suns were low in the sky as Sara checked the straps of the backpack Foster had given her one last time, before slinging it over her shoulder. It contained a small med-kit, a space blanket, and a few packets of food, things she might need. She had gotten in a two-hour nap after the Professor and the lieutenant had left the second time.

She planned to be miles away when the first moon rose. The Eade. Davad and she used to play hide and seek in that area and it would be fitting to play the game there with those the Priests sent out. Perhaps Davad had known this would happen and had prepared her. Besides the Eade was closer to the main temple where the challenge would take place. The Eade had caves where the rock poked up through the jungle floor and was unstable ground which would cause trouble for her pursuers more than her since she had intimate knowledge of its lay. Most of the natives, especially the priests, keep away from the area. Davad never really told her why.

Slipping silently through the forest/jungle, she kept up a situational awareness. It wouldn't do for her to be taken by surprise by Rolad's other companions. She was sure they were going to be hunting her as well as the priests. If they got in each other's way that would be perfect for her, but not for the priests nor the natives on a whole.

And she was sure Rolad would also be hunting her. At least at first. He would have to return for the Ritual so he could be the champion if she showed up. They had to at least look like they were following the Laws. Or the Laws as the Priests interpreted them. The Laws seemed fluid when the priests needed them to be.

Now there were devout priests, don't get her wrong but on the whole the Priests were corrupt. They needed a shaking up.

A familiar sound caused her to stop and raised her arm. Caer carefully landed on her forearm and gave a chirp-like noise. Sara scratched his head and tried to project her emotions towards the hawk. She needed him to not give away her location to her pursuers so she wanted him to just stay away for the next three days.

The natives had bred several of the animals for intelligence and domesticallity to make them hunting companions but Priests were not allowed such things. Priests had to be free to form bonds with Degar should he chose to manifest as a "familiar". Degar's lexicon spoke of this "familiar" as the ultimate sign of Degar's blessing but had never manifested though whispered of often by the Priests, especially those who wanted to be the High Priest.

Caer bobbed his head and Sara felt acceptance and sadness projecting from the hawk. Hopefully that meant he knew to stay away for a few days at least. Besides giving her position away, she wouldn't put it past the Priests to kill him to get at her. She flexed her arm and he took to the air. As he flew away, she started moving again, purposely not watching him leave. If everything went right or at least fair for her she would see him again.

Natives in the Priests' employ were no doubt watching and she wanted to make sure they saw her leave the off-world camp. While there were negatives to contact with off-worlders, there were also some positives. Among that there were some that had both. Witness what had started this mess. Introducing the natives to other beliefs and a wider universe was on the whole good because they had been sliding into decline, stagnating, but the Death Cult had taken advantage of the natives' relative nativity. She had been trying to influence the High Priest and some of the apostles through stories she had told. To stir them toward the more positive side of Elgar's religion with a little of the Church's philosophy thrown in here and there. She had seen one civilization destroy itself through intolerance, and she didn't want to see this one fall from within. Or through manipulation by outside forces.

The ground became rocky and she slowed her pace. She was at the far edge of The Eade where it became more junglely and rocks seemingly randomly poked up through the ground. The farther in you went the bigger and more numerous the rocks got and the thinner the jungle flora, though it never cleared completely. Some of the rocks formed caves with vines growing on and covering the rocks, hiding many an entrance to said caves. But she knew almost every inch of this area. Years playing hide and seek and hunting with Davad on this land had made sure of that. Maybe he had realized she would come in conflict with the Priests and had prepared her for this.

It was growing darker. The suns would be down soon and the Hunt would begin with the moons rise. Rolad and the off-worlders were no doubt already on her trail. But following a trail in The Eade was as hard as the ground. With the moons the night was never truly dark but it was harder to see the minute signs of passage that the rocky ground gave. Rolad was the one she was the most worried about. He knew this area also, though not as much as Davad had. Though skilled with the local weapons, the priests were not skilled hunters or trackers. Most spent very little time outside their temples, much less civilized areas. Apostles did but if they made the grade to priest, they too stopped. The old saying that power corrupts seemed to be true with the priests.

She slipped around a rock and slid sideways into a crack. Two steps and she was in a small cave. It was eight feet tall and ten by ten with a small hole in the ceiling and another crack at the back. This would be a good place to wait out the moons rise. She needed a plan bigger than just evading her pursuers.

Sighing, she sat crossed legged by the crack she had entered through. Playing hide and seek with them would only get her so far and put her on the defensive. She needed to keep them awake and moving as well. Apprehensive. Killing them wasn't something she really wanted to do but if she had to she wouldn't have any regrets. She had to survive to get to the challenge. Surviving the challenge was a whole other thing. Even with her advantages she was still human and sleep deprivation affected her though not as much or as soon. But three days was her limit.

Rolad had probably told his uncle some lie about Davad's death. That is if he had told them anything at all. If she hadn't taken care of the body, he probably would have stirred up the Clan with visuals and more lies. He had been jealous of Davad.

Voices came from outside and she tilted her head. Sounded like they were coming closer. She couldn't make anything out yet but it seemed like two voices were arguing. They passed and headed away, but she heard more than two footfalls pass by. Only a few words had reached her but it was enough to tell that it was off-worlders out there. No stealth either. If they continued like that she could easily evade the four she heard go by if she wanted to. Hopefully they stuck together for a bit. Separate they would be easier for her to take out but harder to follow. She would have no problem with killing them as they were a threat to this planet. If only she could make the Priests see that.

Well, if she survived everything maybe she would.

She glanced up at the hole in the ceiling, noting the darkened sky, and stood. It was time.

Slipping out the crack, she glided into the jungle/forest and set a northerly course. The main temple was northeast of here so north was as good as any heading. A few yards that way and her bracer sparkled and tingled. Someone was ahead. She turned more easterly and slowed her pace as she glided from tree to tree, her eyes scanning her surroundings while her hearing flared outward.

The jungle/forest was in twilight, full of dark shadows, but her eyes and hearing were like those of a jungle predator. She moved, glided, like one. The Laren were masters at genetic manipulation and biomechanics and even after years of lapsed practice she was still at the top of her game. Though it was really not a game.

Movement caused her to pause and her bracer tingled and sparked. Something was ahead and to the left in shadow.

She crouched in her own shadow as her awareness sought out what it was. By clothing it was a priest. He was kneeling and studying the ground. Maybe the off-worlders had gone that way or one of the few animals that called this place home. Whatever it was he soon stood and moved off away from her. She waited a few more minutes, then headed off herself, keeping more to the shadows than she had been. If one priest was here then so were the others. She still had a ways to go before she was on the ground she wanted.

The moons moved slowly across the sky as she glided through the jungle/forest. Only the mountains were not covered by the jungle/forest of this planet.

There were two oceans but most of the planet was made up of two giant landmasses. And those landmasses were full of trees similar to oaks, but growing between and amongst those trees were vines similar to those of a Terran jungle. Other jungle vegetation was also abundant, but the experts say it isn't really a jungle. The natives call it a forest. Sara just called it the jungle/forest. There were a few cities, carved out of the jungle/forest, mostly at the edges of where the mountains and hills met the trees while villages or communities were dotted throughout the jungle/forest where Clans had set up. No one had settled in The Eade. The ground rumbled and it was too close to what the natives called The Seat of Delgar. A volcano in actuality. So she was not worried about running into any one but the priests and the off-worlders, another reason she chose this place besides knowing it well.

Evading the priests and Rolad was what she had planned to do but thinking about it she may have to kill them along with the off-worlders. She planned to stalk the off-worlders and kill them if she got the opportunity, but the priest may try to attack her while she did so and she would react accordingly. So she would just have to accept that she may have to kill them all. Rolad would only be hunting for a day as he had to be ready for the Ritual tomorrow evening, giving her only a small window to kill him before the challenge.

What looked like a tumble of large boulders appeared ahead of her. Vines crisscrossed the rocks and stretched to the surrounding trees, making weird shadows. Sara paused, then ducked under the stretched vines on the left. Just past the vines was a hollow area that was lit dimly by the lichen growing on the exposed inner rock. She dropped down and sat inside the hollow, making sure not to brush the lichen. Sara took a drink from her water bottle as she contemplated her next move.

Rolad was no doubt already hunting her But he was probably searching the well-known places along the equally well-known routes through The Eade. After he had showed her those routes enough for her to know them, Davad had shown her how to make her own way through it without losing her direction which helped her in the rest of the jungle/forest. The Clans knew every inch of their own land but followed the routes in other lands, and the off-worlders only knew the main routes as the natives didn't want the off-worlders wandering their lands unsupervised. She never understood why Davad had taught her the things he did. Most of it was against the native laws but every time she protested he would just say, "attend." So she stopped protesting and learned. It wasn't as if she didn't want to. She just hadn't wanted Davad to get into trouble.

The Priest she had seen earlier had probably been following the off-worlders, but the other

Priests would no doubt survey the routes for her first as well. Off-worlders rarely strayed into the jungle/forest as it was easy to get lost--and injured--if you didn't have experience with jungles or forests. Hopefully the off-worlders and Priests would split up and stake-out different places so she could stalk individuals. After all as the saying goes a good defense is a good offense and taking them out one by one would be better for her. The Priest she had seen had been older at least, so she suspected that the others were older as well since she really didn't have as much trouble with the younger ones. It was mostly the older priests who didn't like off-worlders and were resistant to any change. Perhaps it would be good to rid the priesthood of them.

More green-tinged moonlight crept across in front of her, telling her the second moon was above. Both moons were now high in the sky. The Hunt was now official. It was telling that both parties hadn't waited for the official start. But then she hadn't expected them to. A way of life was in the balance.

FOUR

Recapping her water bottle, she put it away then stood. She needed to recon. Rolad and the Priests should have already staked-out their places. Or at least the Priests would have. She had a feeling Rolad would roam a bit as he knew she wasn't a novice. Perhaps she should follow after the priest she had seen earlier. But she needed to know where all the priests were before she went after the off-worlders. She could really use Caer right now for recon but it was still too risky. So she would just have to rely on her own observations.

She listened for a moment, then stepped out of her hiding place and resumed an easterly heading. If she continued in this direction she would run into one of the routes and she could parallel the route until she spied a priest or an off-worlder. Once she had everyone marked she could began systematically taking them out. That is if everything went well. But Murphy liked to interfere.

Her eyes held a bit of a gleam as she glided through the jungle/forest, even though there was more than enough moonlight to see by. The moonlit night was the same as daylight to her. None of the shadows hid anything from her.

There had been nothing lacking in what the Laren had done to her. They had needed a warrior who was self-sufficient. Sight, hearing, and reflexes were enhanced and hidden bio-mechanical defensive weapons were added to her arsenal of visible weapons. The Laren may have taken most of her visible weapons away when the War ended but they couldn't reverse what they had done physically. And they definitely couldn't take away her memories.

At least not without changing who she was.

Sound turned her attention to some hanging vines and flora just ahead to her right and she paused in shadow. Sparks and tingles flickered through her bracer. Her eyes caught movement and she melted more into the shadows as she zeroed in on said movement.

By clothing the figure squatting in the flora was an off-worlder. His attention was focused ahead. Probably on the route that cut through there. Sara didn't see or hear any other person nearby, though one could be on the other side of the route, of course. Perhaps she should take him out. That way he wouldn't be at her back when she continued on.

The off-worlder cupped his left ear, then muttered something before shifting again. So that told Sara he had a Com. She would have to kill him quick and silently to keep the others from hearing anything. Unless she used her shirikan. It would paralyze both the man and the Com, then she could take her time and question him. Though she figured he wouldn't tell her anything.

Flickering her fingers, an energy shirikan appeared, and she moved carefully until she had a clear shot at him. With a flick of her wrist, the energy flew, and the man fell forward. Checking the surroundings again, she waited a minute before moving to his side and rolling him over. His eyes widened as he saw her and she smiled tightly. "Hi there. Looking for me?"

He couldn't answer of course. The shirikan paralyzed everything but breathing and eyes.

"So I'm going to ask you some yes or no questions. Blink once for yes and twice for no. Do you understand?"

The off-worlder just glared at her.

Sara squatted next to him and began rummaging through his clothing. Besides his blaster, he wasn't carrying much; just some local money, a local guest chip, and his Terran ID. Since she didn't have a reader she couldn't get more than his name from the ID. It said his name was Kevin Anderson. "Well, Mr. Anderson, can't say it's a pleasure. I gather you're a member of the Death Cult or at least working with them."

He continued to just glare at her.

"So as much as I hate to waste life, I can't very well leave you alive." She pulled her round knife from her boot and flicked it open.

His glare got harder and hotter.

"You really can't say anything. You were going to ambush me. That blaster is not set to stun." She watched him swallow and his mouth twitch as if he tried to say something. "I know you'd rather go out in a blaze of glory so Elgar will reward you but you don't deserve a clean death. Elgar would not condone what you're doing, though his priests would. They were the ones that started the Ilan War."

Something flickered in the off-worlder's eyes, even as sparks and tingling flickered across her bracer.

Sara lunged immediately to her right and rolled until she came up in a battle crouch. Her knife flew as soon as she saw the new intruder. It struck home in his heart and he staggered before falling to the ground. When he remained still, she looked over to the off-worlder and saw the dart in his chest. She stood and went over to her kill. He wasn't the priest she had seen earlier and he wasn't wearing priest robes but an apostle's long knee tunic. However he had a priest's symbol hanging around his neck.

Only priests wore that symbol. Apostles had a different symbol. The priest symbol was similar to a Terran pentagram with an eye in the center while the apostle one was just a triangle with a slanted line through it. Once the apostle became a priest he changed from the thin long-sleeved knee-length tunics and linen pants to tailored hooded robes and switched symbols. Apostles did the day-to-day stuff in the temples while the priests performed ceremonies and as judges in higher courts.

Communities had guards and normal courts for normal grievances as well, but priests were the supreme judges.

This priest was older. Probably about fifty. So middle-aged for the natives who lived well into their nineties before age got to them. He probably belonged to the old guard that believed their own hype. The younger priests were generally devote and followed an honorable course, but after years of watching the older priests circumvent the laws, they too gave in and many became corrupt themselves. A few became withdrawn and isolated themselves.

She pulled her knife out and wiped it on the priest's tunic before sheathing it back in her boot. Hooking her arms under his, she dragged him closer to some flora, then rolled him into it. Stepping back, she gave the area a look. Satisfied that unless you were next to the area, you wouldn't see him, she moved over to the off-worlder and repeated the operation. When she was satisfied that he was hidden as well, she nodded to herself and moved away, keeping her eyes peeled for any more people. Though if there had been anyone nearby they would have already arrived.

Two down. Seven to go. In a way she was grateful the priest had showed up; she didn't like to kill in cold blood. It reminded her too much of her past. But she would have done it. When something needed to be done, she did it, not always without regret but she would do it if it was necessary.

Sparks and tingles flickered across her bracer and she melted into a shadow as she stopped. The other creature paused as well. It was a sworlot, a animal that looked like a cross between a Terran sloth and a Terran leopard. Four legged but with the ability to stand two legged and use its front limbs like arms. Sworlots were the top of the food chain of the native animals and virtually untamable. There was only one instance that was recorded of a person having one as a hunting companion.

She took a step forward and met the sworlot's tawny eyes as she flicked a shirikan into being. There was no reason to kill it and if it would walk off she would go her own way. The sworlot held her eyes unblinkingly. They stared at each other for a timeless moment, then Sara allowed her shirikan to dissipate as she stepped back, her eyes still on the sworlot's. A rumble, then the sworlot blinked and glided away. Unfortunately, it was headed the same direction Sara had wanted to go. She adjusted her course slightly and moved out herself. Hopefully she wouldn't run into it again.

The moons moved slowly across the sky as she glided through the jungle/forest, carefully keeping to the shadows now as she was mirroring the main route through The Eade. She was surprised that she had not run into any other person yet, especially Rolad. Of course the way station was still ahead and that was no doubt where most of the off-worlders awaited her. There were two hidden caves ahead as well. She would spend most of tomorrow in one to let the hunters get complacent before she ventured out to hunt them.

INTERVAL

Topaz eyes opened in the dimly lit stasis chamber.

The creature resembled a native sworlot except its face was more humanoid. It sat up and climbed out of the chamber.

Symbols appeared in the air, then a hologram. The hologram ran through the scene of what had happened in the Laren chamber above, causing the creature to growl. More symbols appeared as well as something that looked like a countdown. With a grunt, the creature scampered out of the room into the hallway and moved toward a sealed archway. When the creature got close the archway slid open to reveal a long dark tunnel. The creature entered and the door slid shut leaving it in darkness as the creature moved forward.

Moments later the creature was at the end of the

tunnel and plunged into the moonlit jungle/forest. Behind it there was a rumble and a plume of dust came out of the cave mouth in the cliff wall, raining debris to the ground below.

FIVE

It was well past local midnight when she neared the first of the hidden caves. She did a bit of recon before approaching in closer. Sara barely disturbed the flora as she weaved first left, then right in a crisscross pattern until she squatted where she had a visual on the vine-covered egress.

The area around the hidden cave seemed secure, but sparks and tingles had flickered across her bracer. She had scouted around enough to say no one was hid near this egress so whatever had set off her life detector had to be in the cave or near the other point of egress. It had to be one of the priests or Rolad because the off-worlders wouldn't know of these little caves.

Unless Rolad told them.

But Rolad didn't spend much time in The Eade. He spend more time with the Clan near the Port than anything. When he wasn't working the family business. And the High Priest had supported that. Perhaps there was something more going on than she thought.

"Lendri," Rolad's voice came from the cave. "I know you're out there."

Sara didn't say anything but she readied a dart and her blow tube in case he got stupid and showed himself.

"You weren't the only one he showed his secrets."

She remained silent and poised. Like the cave she had used earlier this one had a 'back door' so she figured he would use that as an egress. Especially if one of his off-worlder 'friends' was watching that exit. She could always take that 'friend' out. However she decided to remain where she was, at least for the moment.

"I regret that I won't be around when the off-worlders kill you," he continued. "But I must begin to set up the 'dominoes'."

Her temper flared, but Sara bit her lip and remained quiet. She knew he was baiting her. Whether to get her to give her position away or to make her angry enough to do something else stupid she wasn't sure.

"No comment?" He laughed harshly. "It's inevitable that the Cult takes this planet. Degar is after all an off-shoot of Elgar. And you don't think this is the only planet in the Cult's sight do you? As soon as they take control the word will be given and the others will fall."

That was what she feared. If they took

Greenpeace, it was but a stepping stone and they would take the other planets that worshiped a similar entity, then try to take over the whole of the Federation. Sparking another holy war that would pit brother against brother, sister against sister and lead up to genocide again. Suicide bombers. How many had the off-worlders tainted already?

"I'll take Uncle's place here with the new order."

A new surge of anger flashed through her, but she remained silent. He was totally corrupted by the off-worlders. She had hoped there was something to redeem in him, even after he had killed Davad.

"Still nothing? How disappointing."

Now she was sure he was trying to have her give away her position. One of the off-worlders must be here if not two or all three. She really needed to question one of them about their plans, but she feared she would have to act too aggressively to do so. And maybe these were just fodder and didn't know the whole plan.

"I've wasted enough time here. I need to get back. I'm sure the off-worlders will take good care of you, Lendri, so goodbye."

Silence reigned after that and Sara figured he left through the back egress. She waited for a few minutes, then carefully straightened from her crouch. Sparks and tingles warned her and she lunged, tackling the off-worlder who appeared on her left into the tree he had just come around. She whirled him around and forced his arm behind his back even as she twisted the blaster from his hand. Her own weapon lay on the ground where she had dropped it when she had lunged.

The off-worlder grunted as he was slammed back into the tree.

"What's this plan Rolad was alluding to?"

A curse was her only answer.

Sparks and tingles warned her a second before she heard the second off-worlder. She lunged to the side and rolled away from the off-worlder she held. Continuing to her feet, she glided off deeper into the jungle/forest, hoping to lose any followers. Hearing no one on her trail, she slowed and turned back toward her original course. She didn't really want to engage them right now or she would have confronted both of them. There was a slim chance that she would have been injured if she had and that was unacceptable right now.

She would make it to the other hidden cave soon. That cave she was sure neither Rolad nor the off-worlders knew about as she had found it last year and Davad had stated he had never knew of its existence. It was smaller, barely big enough for two people and had only the one egress, but it was well hidden amongst the flora. She could hide there for a few hours of the day at least. Let the off-worlders and priests chase their tails for a while before she actively hunted them. It was better odds for her if she could catch them singlely.

Her bladder made her stop for a minute beside a bush before she continued on. She didn't want to have to go while she was in the cave. Luckily the Laren had been very efficient with that as well when they messed with her body.

A few minutes later what looked like a clump of vines and ferns appeared to her right and she moved toward them. As soon as she reached it, she swept aside some of the vines to reveal a large dark entrance. She carefully entered, allowing the vines to close back behind her as she took two more steps forward. Turning, she dropped to the ground and sat cross-legged in the semi-dark. Hopefully no animal had made this their den or she'd be in trouble come morning.

The predators roamed the night when it was relatively cool in the jungle/forest, hoping to catch any wanderers. Most animals stayed undercover during most of the hot muggy day to escape the heat, and during the middle of the night when the predators roamed. But every creature had to eat and drink. Sworlots and the snake-like Moannos liked these vine-covered caves. She didn't need a run-in with either in this cave.

Pulling off her backpack, she set it in her lap and dug through it until she felt a trail mix bag. Foster had included three of them besides two redi-meals as well as another larger water bottle. She would have to repay him, if she survived. Opening the mix bag, she ate a handful of the nutrient-rich mix. While not delicious it was flavorful.

Better than what the Laren had. Their nutrient-rich redi-meals were bland. They didn't eat for enjoyment but to keep their bodies healthy. Their society was rich in aesthetics like art and books but they neglected things that had to do with the body except modifications to said body. It was contradictory in a way. They took great pleasure in modifying DNA and adding biomechanicals but ignored things like fashion and culinary pursuits.

She hadn't understood a lot about them but she did understand why they had stood against the Cren.

All the normal night noises went silent as a roaring howl broke the night air. A sworlot had killed something. And close by if Sara guessed right by the loudness of the sound.

She put the mix bag back in the backpack and sipped a bit of water before slipping the pack back on her shoulder.

The moons would be dipping beyond the horizon about now and the jungle/forest would be darker for a few hours before the first of the suns would slip up the horizon. As soon as it hit the horizon, she would use the few hours before it got too muggy to do a little hunting or at least recon. The priests would be searching for a cool spot to while away the day either now or at dawn, but she had a feeling the off-worlders would be stumbling around in the heat searching for her. Off-worlders always kept to their day schedules even through the heat. Stupidity or arrogance, maybe both.

It would be easy to hunt the off-worlders during the day. The heat would slow them down and mess with their minds, making them irritable. If they weren't separate they would be by midday from irritability with each other. She should be able to pick them off if they were separated. So her plan was still a go. At least toward the off-worlders.

The priests would be a bit harder. Though they now spent little time in the jungle/forest, they used to when they were younger and you never really lose the knowledge just the physical practice. And stamina. After she took care of the off-worlders she could just play hide and seek with the priests, evading them until she had to go to the main temple. They would get frustrated before her, but they would also get more rest than her as they could sleep away the day where she had to be vigilant so no one could sneak up on her. The priests could always decide to hunt her during the day to keep her off balance. If they were hunting her separate, that was one thing but if they were coordinating, she'd have more trouble. She just wished she knew what they were going to do so she could plan accordingly.

Of course during the War she had had to do most of her planning on the fly. The Cren were nothing if not unpredictable . Some of what they did was controlled by instinct but they were sentient beings with a streak of cunning that rivaled human cleverness. But they didn't think quick on their feet or at least not as quick as humans. Sara had used that to her advantage many times.

She would meditate until the suns started to rise, then do her recon. There was no reason for her to be out there now. Let the off-worlders stumble around and the priest waste their time hunting for her. She could while away the next few hours with contingency plans while her body rested.

Her eyes closed and she sunk into her thoughts, leaving her hearing open to listen for intruders.

SIX

The second sun had just touched the horizon when Sara had left the hidden cave. She glided through the jungle/forest carefully, looking and listening for any movement. While her bracer would warn her if something was close, it couldn't tell her where or how many. It was mainly just an early warning system.

She was headed mainly in the direction she had heard the sworlot from last night. It might have run into the off-worlders or the priests. Besides that would be a good place to start her own hunting. The roar had come from the direction of the main route so it was conceivable that either the off-worlders or the priests had been hunting her there.

A whirl of breeze brought a familiar sickly sweet odor to her. Blood. And nearby, by the strongness of the odor. She slowed her pace and followed her nose.

Moments later she rounded a tree and stopped as she had found the source of the smell. A body slumped against a tree in front of her. It was tore open. All of its inners were flung about the area, blood was dripping everywhere. She had never seen a sworlot do that before, and she knew a sworlot had been here because next to the body was a clear sworlot print in blood. The body had unmistakable claw marks as well.

On the ground to the right was a broken blaster. By what had remained of the clothes she had figured it was an off-worlder. How he had gotten the blaster past the Port Guard she didn't know. They scanned for such things

She scouted the perimeter. Bloody boot prints heading away showed there had been more here than just the dead man so at least one got away. If the sworlot hadn't gone after them that is. She had also found a broken dart so at least one of the priests had still been following them. Maybe he'll go after the sworlot and leave off hunting her.

So that left two off-worlders for her to take care of, if the sworlot didn't take care of them, and at least one priest, if he was still following them. Hopefully the sworlot wouldn't bother her.

The main route was about fifty yards from here but the trail wasn't headed that way. It was going toward the east, but the main route was more north. She decided to follow the trail as long as she could. The off-worlder(s) may have just ran in whatever direction was clear and may have gotten lost, though if they have a compass then finding the correct heading wouldn't be hard. Of course it all depended on their experience with jungles or forests.

And if the priest was inclined to help them.

Skirting the blood, she followed the trail leading away from the scene. She stayed just close enough to see the trail but far enough to the side that she wouldn't run headlong into either the priest or the off-worlder(s). That would definitely ruin her day. One way or the other. The blood faded after a bit but she caught sight of the trail enough to follow for a while. However, those sign too faded after a bit, and she stopped.

They had kept the easterly direction for a while but then had turned north. She had been paralleling the main route for the last hour. They must have entered the main route around here. The priest probably followed them, though he no doubt kept to the jungle/forest. There was a way station about a mile ahead. It was a logical spot for them to stay, at least for a bit, especially if they thought to catch her there. The priests might even be there if they were stupid enough to think of her as a typical off-worlder guest.

She continued to parallel the route, but she was more cautious. The priests or off-worlders could be anywhere, waiting.

Sparks and tingles warned her and she paused, half hidden by flora. Her eyes immediately spotted the movement. A priest was squatting at the edge of the flora, looking into the route. All his attention was there so he had not seen her yet, but if she moved he would either hear her or see her out of the corner of his eye. She had to strike first and decisive.

But before she could move, the priest stepped out of the flora and into the route. Sara slid through the flora to where he had been and looked into the route.

Two off-worlders stood before the tree-bound way station. The priest was standing in front of them, speaking. Sara could hear his voice but not the words themselves. It seems the off-worlders didn't agree with what the priest was saying because they were shaking their heads. The priest spoke again, then headed down the route when both off-worlders nodded. They watched the priest leave, then argued amongst themselves for a minute before one of them went the way the priest had. The off-worlder left behind had his left arm in a rough sling and was bleeding through the material of the sling. He had obviously been there when the sworlot had attacked.

Sara had lost her dart tube so she couldn't just shoot the off-worlder with a dart. And she didn't know if he had a blaster like the other one had. Snapping her fingers, a shirikan sprang into being and with a flick of her wrist, she let it fly. It hit him in the chest above his heart, causing him to fall to the ground. So close to the heart, the small electrical charge it carried should have killed him, but Sara stepped out of the flora onto the route and over to him to check.

The second she knelt over the slumped form, a blaster bolt shot over her where her heart would have been if she was standing. She lunged, rolling away from the fallen off-worlder and behind the tree the way station was on. It had been a trap. She had to get out of here.

A roaring howl, then a scream filled the air. The surviving off-worlder staggered into view, firing his blaster behind him at the sworlot that followed him. Claws had raked him across the back and blood was making the ground slippery for him but he kept firing. Two darts stuck out of the sworlot's shoulders, but it didn't seem to slow it down as it stalked the off-worlder.

GO

The word appeared in Sara's mind. It startled her for a second, then she followed the directive and slipped further into the jungle/forest. She kept an ear and eye out for the priest in case he left the off-worlder on his own to hunt her as she moved northeasterly. After all she wanted to stay on track toward the main temple, and there was a hidden cave not too far this way. She needed time to think without distractions.

Vine-choked rocks rose to her right and she turned toward them. She carefully separated some vines to reveal a space between two tall rocks and slipped inside it. There was just enough room to sit cross-legged in the space which she did. The vines fell back into place, hiding the little cave-like area, and she sighed. Her thoughts were in chaos.

That word had obviously come from the sworlot. Normal sworlots were not intelligent. Facts.

Another fact was that there was a Laren science outpost on this planet. No telling what the Laren did to the native animals. The Laren didn't believe in slavery, but they thought nothing of changing the very DNA of other beings, most of the time without the being's permission. All in the name of improvement, of course. They were an odd, complicated species.

Now that she had time to reflect, she realized the sworlot had had more humanoid features. And the eyes had been more brown than amber. The Laren had definitely messed with its DNA. Unless it was what the original sworlots were and the ones running around were the experiments. The Laren had no compunction about reversing natural selection if it suited them. As Sara had said the Laren were a complicated race. They would do things that they would condemn another race for. All for the greater good, of course.

She had to figure out her next move. Should she remain here for the day or should she move on for a bit and rest during the hottest part of the day in another cave closer to the main temple. Would the sworlot follow her or stalk the priests? What was its intent?

The sworlot had seemed to be on her side earlier. It was going after her enemies anyway, and had told her to go. What was its intent?!

Too agitated to remain sitting, she stood. If she was hunting she could remain still for hours but this was different.

Sunlight came spotty through the vines above, telling her that the one sun was reaching its zenith. In two hours the other would, then it would be too hot to travel too far. She decided to head north to the Orein Waterfall. There was a cave there behind the falls. She didn't think the priests would head there. They wouldn't think she knew about it. Off-worlders didn't. The falls were near the volcano and since that was sacred ground off-worlders were prohibited. Of course the jungle/forest was thin there, but she could weather tomorrow there before heading toward the main temple. She had the food in the backpack and the falls for water. Tonight she could travel. But for now she could head for another cave further north.

Her mind was still spinning with thoughts, but she pushed them aside for now. She was still too close to the earlier conflict and needed to put some distance between it and her. Pushing aside the vines, she slide out of the space. No sparks or tingles and she didn't sense anyone around so she glided toward the north.

SEVEN

Both suns were at their zenith, and the air was muggy enough to choke before Sara reached the cave she wanted. It really was little more than three large rocks leaning against each other but it was shelter. A small breeze whispered through and Sara sighed as she slid past the vines into the slightly cooler cave. That breeze made it more than bearable.

Sitting cross-legged with her back against the cool rock, Sara sat her backpack in her lap and drank some water. She still had the bigger bottle in the pack, but this bottle was almost gone.

There was a small hole dug in the opposite corner for latrine duty. Davad and her had dug it the last time they had come this way. The lack of smell meant no one else had been here since.

This cave was large enough for ten people to

sleep. Most of these hidden caves were only big enough for two. The scientists had many theories about The Eade, but since off-worlders were prohibited, none had ever studied it. Large rocks sprouted like weeds in The Eade. The ground itself was rocky, making the jungle/forest thinner in this area.

Rain fell all over the planet at strange intervals and intensities. The whole planet was strange. Of course, the Laren may have messed with the whole planet. With their terraforming technology they could have even created this whole planet from a space rock. And populated it with experiments before the Terran colonists had stumbled upon it. Before the War, they could have done that. After, she wasn't sure. When she had seen the abandoned Laren outpost, her outlook on this planet had changed. Things she had taken for natural she now wandered if the Laren had messed with.

Speaking of rain, she could hear it coming down now. These quick showers would come and go in minutes or hours during the day, but the longer rains mostly came at dusk. The intensities of the rains changed constantly. Now that she knew the Laren had had an outpost here, she suspected their hand in the weather patterns as well as other things. She wouldn't be able to prove her suspicions though. They had probably wiped out the computer-like mainframe machine they had used when they left, except maybe a maintenance program. The security protocols had obviously not been working properly as the off-worlders had gained access. Unless they somehow had an over-ride of some sort.

She would have to look into that after the challenge, if she survived. While her body was stronger and faster than a normal human's so was the natives' and, if she didn't use her shirikans, her skill was less than Rolad's with the native weapons. Davad had taught her the basics and practiced with her regularly, but they were not her strong suits. Explosives, blaster, and knives were what she knew best and was expert in their use, especially knives. Knives and hand to hand was what she had been trained in since childhood as Ilan only believed close combat was honorable. The explosives and blaster came with the Federation, and the Laren.

Everything seemed to come back to the Laren. Or more properly the Lar' Ren. In the two thousand years that they've been gone, more than their name had changed. Most Federation people had thought them myths until remnants of their civilization showed up both on their own and in other long-dead civilizations. They were myths to the civilizations now dotting the universe but they had indeed been real. Sara had met several and knew them as flawed as humans, but to the Humans now inhabiting the universe they were gods, the ideal to shoot for. The Laren would have found that attitude amusing, but illogical.

A roaring howl reached her ears.

So the sworlot had survived his meeting with both the off-worlder and the priest. And was hunting. If that was it.

One of the vines swayed from more than the breeze, and a Moanno dropped to the floor in front of Sara. The giant green snake-like creature reared up and flared its hood as it confronted Sara.

A shirikan flickered into being and she threw it to distract the creature as she moved into a crouch.

In a flash the Moanno snapped at the shirikan which harmlessly discharged in the fanged mouth.

Sara flashed her knife to the left, and the Moanno's head and eyes followed it, giving her time to pull out a dart. Slashing at its head, she pushed the dart into its body before flinging herself away from it. She crouched as far from it as she could as it started to flail about.

The Moannos were immune to energy weapons due to their bodies absorbing the energy and dissipating it through their scales. Most natives used axes or spears to the head if they had to kill them. Usually Moannos kept away from inhabited areas and natives usually retreated if confronted in the jungle/forest by these giant snakes. There seemed to be a mutual respect or truce between the natives and the Moannos. Each went about their own business and on the rare occasion they met they would step aside.

With a final twitch, the Moanno lay still.

Keeping her knife at the ready, Sara approached the creature's head. She stabbed the blade down between its eyes strongly, then wiped the knife off on its scales before sheathing it back in her boot. Now she would have to drag it outside somewhere before the predators got the scent of fresh meat. She lifted the large head, hooking her arms around its neck, and tugged it toward the 'back' opening. Moannos would put the Terran anacondas to shame in size; their bodies were as big as two human male's thighs put together and they weighed over five hundred pounds, some as much as a thousand. If she hadn't been enhanced there was no way she could move it.

Once outside the cave she headed towards the west, dragging the Moanno over the rocky ground. Hopefully the priests were all settled in a way station or one of the caves near the main route. She'd be at a disadvantage right now.

When she figured she was far enough away from the cave, she dropped the head and retraced her steps. She couldn't do anything about the trail she had left but hopefully she'd be gone before the priests found it, if they found it. With luck the priests would stay around the main route. Well, except for the one that was with the off-worlder. She didn't know if he survived his meeting with the sworlot, and if he had was he still keen on hunting her.

As soon as she got close to the cave, she scouted around a bit for any other intruders, but didn't see anything so she entered.

She didn't know what shocked her more: The sworlot sitting by her pack or that her life signs detector hadn't tell her it was there.

HE

"What?"

MALE. The sworlot tapped its--his--chest. MALE. HE

"Okay, so you're a male." She cautiously sat down. They were only feet apart as the cave wasn't that big, but it--he wasn't making any aggressive moves. Though his word choices were simple she did not think the sworlot was.

The sworlot dipped his head, then tapped his chest again. ANWAR

"Is that your name?"

He dipped his head again.

"I am known as Lendri here." A tilt of his head made her elaborate. "Ghost"

YOU ARE CHOSEN

"If you mean the Laren messed with me as well, then yes."

The sworlot dipped his head, then got up, moving toward the 'back' opening.

Sara watched him leave, then sighed in relief. That was fascinating. She didn't know what to make of this. Nor of the fact that her life signs detector didn't register him. Things were definitely interesting and promised to be more so as time progressed. It seemed for now the sworlot was on her side, and she hoped it stayed that way. She didn't relish a fight with him. Two Laren experiments should have common ground.

And she had much to do yet. Stop a religious resurgence and try to steer the priests back to their true course. So she had to survive another day.

Tonight she would head toward the waterfall. She could spend the day there, then head toward the main temple at dusk. The hunting priests, those that were left, would no doubt be waiting outside the temple for her, but if she made it inside she had dubious protection. There was no hunting allowed inside the main temple. Only the High Priest could order someone killed in the main temple. Supposedly. So capture maybe. She would have to evade people until the Challenge.

The Challenge.

That was a whole other thing. She would have to fight Rolad with native weapons. Her speed and agility was on par with his, probably better, but her experience with the weapons were not. If she used her shirikans, the priests would say she cheated and kill her out of hand. Her skill with knives translated into sword or dagger fighting, but if Rolad chose the Lon staff…which she figured he would as he knew that was one of her weaker weapons. So was Arkon or double ax fighting.

All natives were trained by the Clans in weapons. Though they didn't use them much, they still maintained the training. It was a hold-over from their ancestors. From before the priests took over completely and settled the Clans down using more fear than respect to do so.

Ilan were taught self-defense from the time they could walk using their bodies as weapons. Knives were added when they reached puberty. Those the Death Cult priests took in got advanced training in both along with their teachings. Blasters were added later when the Cult went against the Church.

The Church. Now there was a true cult. Land on a planet and start converting right away, no matter what the natives believed. They may do a lot of good for the Federation generally, but not always specifically. At least they didn't rule the Federation.

Yet.

Sara was sure that was on their agenda. She relaxed against the wall as best she could. The Church was not something she wanted to think about. It brought up bad memories. She would try and rest a bit. There was a lot of walking to do in her future.

EIGHT

It would soon be dusk. Sara hadn't gotten much rest, her mind kept circling her past. Thus the early leave-time. She had planned to leave just after dusk but she might as well go now since she couldn't rest. Besides she didn't want to be here if the priests found the trail from the Moanno.

Hooking the backpack over her shoulders, she headed off in the direction of the waterfall. The ground would get rockier with more space between the trees the closer she got to the falls. So it would be easier for the priests to spot her if they were hunting that way. The one priest had followed the off-worlders so who's to say one of the others wasn't on her trail now or waiting at the falls?

The sworlot had been a surprise in more than one way. Not truly unpleasant but definitely unexpected. It had knocked her off her stride a bit.

Though after finding the outpost, she should have expected something. The Laren would have left their experiments in stasis when they left, but they also would have set instructions for eventualities. They were a farsighted people.

Was the sworlot shadowing her or stalking the priests?

What did it--he really want?

And…How intelligent was it--he?

She wouldn't be completely settled until she had the answers to those and more questions. But she couldn't let any of this upset her end plan. The Death Cult couldn't get control of this planet or any other planet for that matter. The fighting that would result would rival the War with the Cren and would no doubt end in genocide like Ilan had. Under the Death Cult takeover the older Priests, at least, would have to go, no matter what the Cult told Rolad. And anyone showing the slightest rebellion would have to be harshly punished or killed as well. They would have to do this on every planet they took over.

And the Church wouldn't just let them take over a planet they had one of their covenants on. Greenpeace didn't have a covenant so it was a good choice for the first takeover, but the Cult would eventually if not sooner try to take over a planet with a covenant. Very few of the Federation planets didn't have one.

Then, once the Church was in, the Federation would have to step in itself officially. Civil War. Neighbor against neighbor, planet against planet.

Of course this was years down the road. The Cult

would solidify its hold on each planet before moving to the next step of taking over the universe. Take over Greenpeace and one or two other planets, then solidify before moving on to the next group of takeovers. This strategy had worked before and may work again.

The moons rose, casting light and shadow around her. She was gliding along at a rapid clip. Faster than a walk but slower than a full run. She could keep this pace for hours before she needed to slow down. The Laren had trained her well though not long. Time was a plaything to the Laren, but it had rules that even they had to follow. Fixed points that they could not mess with, but they had worked around. Thus the creation of herself and the others.

Foliage was starting to thin and the trees were further apart, even though she still had a ways to go before she got to the falls. The ground was rockier, but still even enough for her to keep up the pace. When she got closer, she would have to slow to a careful walk as bigger, and more, rocks would pepper the ground. The spotty grass would get even spottier until she reached the falls. Her trail would be even harder to follow than it already was, but if they suspected she was heading for the falls, there were ways the priests could get there before her.

If she could survive the day tomorrow she'd have a chance of at least making it to the challenge. She could leave the falls and shadow the cliff way to the main temple area. The natives and priests wouldn't expect her to take that dangerous a trip. Hopefully there hadn't been a slide or she might have to risk going back and taking one of the routes.

She had to be in the main temple before they closed the main gates at dawn or she'd be late to the challenge and forfeit. Then her guest-right would be denied and she would be outcast. The priests could then take her prisoner and punish her as they saw fit or exile her from the planet if they decided not to kill or imprison her. So she had to be on time. Had she been a native it would be different; Her Clan would keep her safe. Or if Davad had still been alive, he would have defended her guest-right.

Little by little, year after year, the priests had corrupted the original laws that governed them and their flock. Laws that were meant to help now repressed. Davad's uncle being the High Priest had a set of the original laws and scriptures, and many a time Davad had snuck her into his uncle's 'office' so she could view them. Luckily, her memory was picture perfect, literally. She could call up any page and recite it verbatim.

Most times she wished her memory wasn't so sharp. There was a lot she wanted to forget about her past but her mind wouldn't let her. When she was on a mission, she could put things in a mental box and close the lid for a bit, but they always came out again if her mind wandered or the mission ended. Focus was key. These last five years she had been keeping that lid on good with all the stuff Davad had been teaching her about life on this planet, but it had slipped a few times making her depressed when that happened. Davad had always kicked her out of the doldrums, mainly by nearly kicking her ass. He had been almost as good as her with knife fighting. All that practice with her.

She nearly stumbled as the ground changed. Her mind had been too busy with her thoughts to register the change. Good thing the priests hadn't shown up or she may have not noticed them.

Slowing, she cautiously picked her way through and over the very rocky ground. The flora was sparse here, but still present enough to be called part of the jungle/forest. She kept her awareness on the here and now, pushing back everything that didn't pertain to the jungle/forest. There would be time to sink into thought once she made it behind the falls

The moons were past their zenith and were rapidly sinking. Well, at least they seem to be as she made slower progress toward the falls. She didn't understand how time did that, but it did. The Laren would know.

She shook her head at the stray thought.

Ground dropped away ahead of her, and she stopped at the edge to look down. Water cascaded just below her and disappeared into a mist further down. To her right was a rock face, then another waterfall. These were the Orein Waterfalls.

There was handholds in the rock face between the falls that went all the way to the bottom. No one knew who put them there but they were the only way down. Besides taking the risk with the waterfall itself. Miles to the east there was a basket to lower people and cargo that was built long ago, but otherwise the land below was inaccessible. Well, except by off-worlder air car. The few Clans that had settled the lowland below were rarely seen and mostly forgotten by the main highland Clans.

She debated briefly with herself, but decided it

was worth it, and swung the pack off her shoulders. Opening it, she pulled out her cloak, then swung the pack back on her shoulders before slipping on the hooded cloak. When she hit the falls, it would keep her dry from the water though it would also get in her way as she climbed. Kneeling, she turned her back to the falls and, holding her breath, slipped over the edge. She found the holds immediately and let out a gust of air in relief. They were dry up here but the further down she went the wetter they would be.

Moving cautiously she climbed down. There was a ledge just inside the mists that lead into the caves behind the falls. It also lead off toward the main temple on the other side of the one fall. That's the way she would take tonight.

The holds indeed got slippery and she slowed down even more. It would be the height of stupidity if she made it this far and fell because she wasn't paying attention. Water gathered on her cloak as she entered the mist proper and she was glad she had it on since it would keep her mostly dry. Her front was getting wet from contact with the rock face as she moved down but her head and back were staying dry, even though the wind was whipping her a bit.

Her right foot hit the edge of the ledge, and she slid over to get on it properly. It was only three feet wide right here, though it only increased another foot on the other side of the fall. She hugged the wall and kept sliding until she passed through the water of the falls to where the cave opened up. Two steps forward and she was in a large dim cavern with the waterfall at her back. The moonlight shining through the water gave her enough light to see.

Stalagmites and stalactites littered the cavern but there was a small clear area back a ways and to the right which could be used for a camp. She shook off her hood and headed there. Once she was at the clear area, she took off her wet cloak and hung it on one of the nearest small stalagmites. She wasn't going to put it away wet, only to get it out again when she left. Not to mention getting the pack and contents wet. Slipping off the pack, she dropped cross-legged to the floor before settling the pack in her lap. She was safe enough here, if the priests hadn't followed her, and could wait out the day in this cavern.

Barely over the roar of the falls, she could make out a roaring howl. It had to be close if she could hear it over the sound of the rushing water. Well, that answered that. Someone had followed her.

But it sounded like the sworlot was hunting whomever it was.

That is if that was Anwar.

Sara slumped. She could do nothing more than wait.

NINE

Sara stepped out onto the ledge, heart pounding, her cloak and hood upon her. She slid along the side of the waterfall and exited into the mist. Her hands skimmed the wall face as she continued along the ledge, facing the rock but head turned enough to see ahead. It would be faster if she turned and walked, but the sight would cause her to panic. She had never lost her fear of heights but she had to do this.

The High Priest and Rolad knew this so they would not expect her to take this way to the main temple. But it was the best way to get there in her time frame with the least chance of running into her hunters. It was almost a straight line to the temple.

And dusk had just begun so she was not that much in a hurry. If she kept a steady pace and didn't run into too much trouble, she would make it to the main temple just as the moons passed their zenith. If she kept her cloak on and up, she should be able to pass right into the temple without anyone the wiser.

She slid along the ledge as fast as she dared. Her vision was limited with the mist surrounding her but the way was clear enough, though slippery. Hopefully there was no slide or erosion anywhere along the ledge which would block the way. She was now committed to this route. Coming back and going over land would take too long, and her petition would be forfeited. That couldn't happen. Too much rode on her at least making it to the challenge.

Winning would be preferable. But Rolad and most of the natives had a leg up on her concerning weapons. The Laren had made her a good commando, but she was no weapons master. She was good ; She had survived the War after all, but she had her weaknesses. And the native weapons were one of them. Her agility might give her time to find Rolad's.

The mists abruptly ended and she increased her pace from the crawl it had been. Moonlight lit the ledge ahead but the unevenness of the cliff wall did not increase visibility very much. Except downward. She kept her eyes straight along the cliff wall, not letting them drop. If she looked down, she knew she would freeze. The ledge was sturdy and wide enough and she knew her balance was excellent, but then fear was unreasonable.

Fear in battle was one thing, but her fear of heights was another.

Water or something had worn away most of the

ledge ahead. She carefully slid into that section, hugging the wall as hard as she could, but could feel the heels of her feet hang over the edge. Slowing and balancing on her toes, she moved carefully along the uneven stone. A few minutes later, the ledge was back to its full size and she sighed before picking up her pace again as she headed on. She knew there would be more tight spots, but she hoped there wouldn't be any breakage. The wall didn't have much in the way of holds, and, depending on how wide the break, she might not be able to jump it.

She almost fell into a sort of rhythm as she moved along the ledge. There were a few tight spots here and there as she, and the time, moved on, but nothing as extreme as that first one and she almost relaxed after a while.

Which is when she spotted the break.

It was in the curve of the ledge ahead so the extent was not foreseeable. The wall was rough with a sharp curve going back, and the area looked as if something had chiseled the ledge off. She stopped at the break and tried to see around the curve as much as she could but that proved useless since she was too far away. The wall face was rough and she could see a chunk of the ledge just at the apex of the curve so she decided to try climbing the wall. She had to make it to the challenge so she would take the risk.

Her right hand reached out and felt along the wall just above her head. She found a hold and allowed her body to hang from her one hand while her foot searched for a toe hold. When she found one, she eased her weight on the foot and exchanged her left hand for her right. If she couldn't find a toe hold she switched hands carefully, hanging from them until she found a toe hold. She did this until she made it to the chunk of ledge at the middle of the curve.

What she saw on the other side of the curve wasn't encouraging.

The wall itself was sheer, and the ledge was totally gone around the rest of the curve. A crumbling edge was about a hundred feet ahead, but jumping from a standstill was of course problematic.

However she didn't have much of a choice.

She carefully pulled off her pack and just as carefully removed her cloak before shoving it into the pack. When it was zipped close, she slipped the pack back on securely. With a hand on the wall, she crouched on the edge of the chunk of ledge, facing the edge of the ledge a hundred feet ahead. Taking a deep breath, she sprang.

As she left the chunk she already knew she was going to miss. At least with her feet. She stretched out and landed belly first on the edge. Her hands scrabbled as she slid down, tearing her nails and skin but stopping her movement. She breathed for a moment, then wiggled onto the ledge. That had been close, too close.

When she could move without risking a fall, she got up to a kneeling position and looked at her hands. Scrapes, dirt, and blood littered her palm. She pulled off her pack and got out the larger bottle of water. After taking a drink, she rinsed the blood and dirt from her hands to examine the wounds. Two were deeper but the rest were superficial. They were okay enough to do without bandaging.

She took another drink and put the bottle back in the pack before standing. The pack went on her back and she hugged the wall again. She set off at a steady pace, slower than before but still a fast clip. This break had set her back a bit on her time table.

Time seemed to speed by as the moons kept moving through the sky. She rounded a curve and saw the lift basket station and the main temple ahead.

The station and temple had been built into the cliff wall. Though the temple ranged from the ledge upwards to three stories above the edge, the station set on the ledge and opened into a steep staircase with the basket itself going all the way to the ground below the cliff.

And basket was a misnomer. It was the size of a small one room house and could carry cargo as well as humans up the side of the cliff wall.

She pulled off her pack and removed her cloak. She swung the pack on her back, then slipped on the cloak. It should help her pass into the temple without too much notice. She could see the basket coming up. Maybe she could slip in with them.

Her pace picked up and she made it to the station just as the basket docked. She slipped in behind the two that stepped off the basket onto the ledge and entered the station with them. A staircase led upward to the left and double doors stood at the back. Two rooms and a counter to the right. She headed for the double doors while the other two headed for the stairs. They must be headed for the town that grew in a half circle around the protective wall of the main temple. Sara needed to be in the temple before the gates in that protective wall were closed and these doors were locked. The Priests prayed and slept during the day, then did their priestly duties at night. Suitable for a death deity followers.

She strode confidently toward the doors and opened them, stepping just inside. The doors closed behind her, and she turned her full attention to the corridor ahead of her. Stairs led upward at the end, and four doors lined the left side. She noticed signs next to the doors, and moved to see what the signs said in the dim light. The last one had the signs for kitchen and supply. So it should lead to the kitchen's supply rooms which would be a good place to hide until the challenge.

Boots on the stair caused her to open the door and slip inside the small dim room. Stairs in the center of the room led upwards, and she followed them.

TEN

The stairs led to a small room with two regular doors and a pair of swinging doors. She had figured the swinging doors were to the kitchen and the others the supply rooms so she had taken one of the regular doors. It had opened into a segregated cavern full of various food items and she picked an out of the way place to wait.

At the time she figured dawn had come, a priest had entered the cavern, but he didn't stay long or look around, just did his business and left. She had ventured out a few hours later and was lucky enough to find a necessary and an empty prayer cell on the next level. There was a priest robe hanging on the back of the door and she had taken it.

Now she was on the ground floor of the temple, heading down one of its corridors. She had to be in the courtyard within the hour, but she was unsure of the layout of this place. The other temples were supposed to have the same layout as this main temple but there were more corridors in this one-- and stairs. She hoped she had taken the right corridors when she had gotten off the last staircase or she would be heading in the wrong direction.

A pair of double doors came up on her left and she stopped. This should lead into the main Hall which in turn opened into the courtyard. She opened the doors and stepped inside, allowing the doors to close behind her.

Before her was the back of a enormous statue of Degar. An altar set in front of the statue with two stairs before it leading down to a large open space. On the other side of the cavern were two glass doors set in a glass archway. There were carvings all over the walls, but Sara was too far away from most of them to see what they were. The ones next to her that she could see were of Degar in different poses so she suspected the other carvings were more of the same.

She rounded the statue and headed for the doors. Rolad was probably already out in the courtyard with a selection of priests. The High Priest would have selected priests who wanted to keep the status quo but Rolad no doubt slipped in some who wanted a closer relationship with the off-worlders, specifically the Death Cult. She would have to watch her back.

At the doors, she paused and studied what she could see of the courtyard. It was about two acres wide and three acres long with the temple on one side and the stone wall enclosing it on three sides.

The far side had an enormous metal gate and stone guardhouse. Priests stood in groups around the courtyard with the High Priest and Rolad waiting in the center, facing the closed gate.

Sara carefully slipped out of the temple and made her way toward the High Priest and Rolad. It was close to time. She stopped a few yards from them and cleared her throat.

Both whirled around.

She shook the hood off and gave them a tilt of her head.

"So you made it," Rolad commented.

Another tilt of the head but no words.

"Sworlot got your tongue?" Rolad asked with a raised eyebrow.

Sara removed the robe, allowing it to drop to the ground, then turned to the High Priest. "High Priest Nuet, I am here to claim challenge as requested."

"Guest Sara Conner, it is granted. Brother Rolad, if you will." The High Priest stepped back and the other priests formed a large circle as Rolad gestured toward a priest holding two Lon staffs.

"I choose Lon staffs."

The staffs were about five feet long with a metal ball on one end and a blade on the other. Most priests carried them when they traveled as apostles. Rolad was proving his own point with this choice.

She accepted the staff from the priest and hefted it a bit to get its weight, then whirled it once. It was heavier than the one Davad had trained her with. Rolad had probably added lead to it. That was a common hazing trick. He meant for her to lose one way or another.

Rolad gave her a smirk.

Dropping the pack on top of the robe, she loosened her shoulders before moving to stand in front of Rolad with the staff gripped in both hands. She knew he would try to keep her on the defensive until he wore her down or broke through, but she planned to turn the tables on him. The staff may be one of her weaknesses but she had stamina and agility.

And she planned to anger the priests so if she lost, the Cult would not have an easy victory. If Rolad got angry as well, all the better.

The High Priest clapped his hands together and stepped back into the crowd.

Rolad swung out but Sara caught it and danced away. They traded some blows as they circled, getting the feel of each other. Rolad landed a blow across her ribs and Sara felt a sharp pain, knowing he cracked a rib, but she danced away without a wince.

"Did you tell your father that you killed Davad?" she asked as she danced away from another swing.

"If Davad is dead, it is your fault." Rolad returned as he swung again.

"Did your friends tell you that you would be High Priest if you helped them?" She spoke loud enough so those in the first row would hear her, including his uncle the current High Priest.

Rolad threw a fury of blows at her, but she managed to avoid most of them by blocking with her own staff. She threw her own blows at his mid section and managed to hit him before she had to dance away from another of his blows.

"Did they tell you that they would have to kill the older priests to ensure their takeover?"

With an angry shout, Rolad lunged at her, whirling his staff.

Sara stumbled back, tripping and landing on her butt, but blocking the blow heading for her head. She kicked him in the solar plexus and leaped to her feet, delivering a blow to his side before he regained his control. He limped, but she knew better than to think he was wounded enough to give her an advantage. Her own body was hurting but she too could carry on.

He attacked her again and she had to retreat a few steps before she could dance away. Her agility gave her an advantage of dodging some of his attacks, but her lack of experience handicapped her. Neither of them were getting anywhere. This fight could last a long time unless one of them made a mistake.

"You know you're just going to be their puppet, don't you?" She told him. "You're just to appease the Clans enough so they won't fight the change. As soon as they have this planet firmly in their grasp, you'll be disposed for one of their own."

"You don't know what you're talking about," he growled.

"None better," she returned as she dodged a blow. "I was once a member."

"Blasphemer," he yelled as he lunged at her again.

This time his blow landed but she managed to dance away before he could make another swing. "Truth. I was Ilan." Her words made him freeze for a second and she scored a hit before they both danced away.

She could hear the priests muttering amongst themselves. Her words were at least reaching them, and Rolad growled before lunging at her. His staff's blade hooked behind her knee as he swept it at her and sliced her, making her stumble. She fell to her knees but blocked the following blow. They stayed in that position, staring at each other.

Rolad's eyes were dilated, and Sara knew he was on the Cult's designer drug. Which explained why none of her hits beside the shot to the solar plexus seemed to affect him. It turned pain into pleasure but depleted the body's moisture. The risk of death was high, but many Cultist thought that it was worth that risk. Rolad's off-worlder friends had probably not told him what he risked.

"You have lost," she told him in a soft voice. "You may kill me but I have planted what I needed to. The priests will not trust you or your off-worlder friends. Not even your Uncle."

He knocked her staff away and shoved her to the ground. His staff's blade rested at her throat, but he did not kill her. He raised his eyes and looked at the priests that surrounded them.

She knew what he was seeing by the look on his face.

"Hold!" a voice called out.

Rolad growled but before he could move a priest grabbed his staff. They stared at each other, neither backing down.

Sara recognized the priest as the one who had been following the off-worlders. He jerked the staff away from Rolad and grounded it next to him, causing Sara to go limp in relief. She had a reprieve, at least for now.

"Brother Janks." The High Priest stepped forward to acknowledge the priest.

"Your Highness." The priest, Janks, didn't take his eyes off Rolad. "I request a stay."

The High Priest tilted his head. "A Stay."

"Yes, your Highness."

"Hmm." The High Priest stared at Janks for a moment, then nodded. "Granted."

"Thank you, your Highness."

"Champion Rolad, please stand down." The High Priest looked at Rolad who didn't move. "Champion Rolad."

Rolad grabbed his staff and shoved Janks away, but Sara had rolled and gotten to her feet before he could turn the weapon on her. He whirled the staff and lunged at her, but missed as she danced away.

Before he could go after her again four priests jumped him and wrestled him to the ground.

Eleven

A roaring howl echoed in the courtyard. Priests scrambled out of the way as something made its way from the outer wall toward the group wrestling with Rolad.

As the priests opened the way, Sara saw why. It was the sworlot Anwar.

The priests wrestling didn't see the sworlot until it was upon them. They too scrambled out of the way, leaving Rolad to get to his knees. He came face to face with the sworlot and they stared at each other, everyone silently watching.

TRAITOR

By the surprised look on Rolad's face, he too had heard the sworlot.

"Yes," Sara nodded. She ignored the questioning looks the High Priest and some of the other priests shot her and kept her attention on the scene before her.

"I am not. Elgar…" His words died as Anwar snarled in his face and he leaned back.

TRAITOR. Anwar repeated the word.

"No." Rolad shook his head

"Yes, "Sara repeated her word.

In a swift move, Anwar ripped out Rolad's throat. As Rolad's body fell to the ground, the sworlot glided over to Sara and sat at her side, his eyes staring out at the priests. He spit out his mouthful at her feet and gave a raspy purr.

"He's yours?" Janks asked in the silence.

"No." Sara shook her head

"This is the second time I've seen him in your company."

"Is this why you asked for the Stay?" The High Priest spoke up.

"Partly, Your Highness." Janks paused. "Off worlders were hunting her. They had blasters."

Angry muttering swept through the priests.

"I wanted to ask her why they would risk so much to kill her."

"Their plans for a takeover were in jeopardy. I had already disrupted those plans by killing the Cultists at the Strader Ruins and they didn't want to take the chance that I would further disrupt or even stop their plans. Rolad was no doubt to start cultivating priests into the plans if he hadn't already."

More, louder, mutterings swept through the Priests.

"How do we know you speak the truth?" a priest called out. "You claim you are Ilan. Everyone knows they genocided decades ago."

"And you're an off-worlder," another said.

"Neither doesn't mean I don't speak the truth about the takeover." She wasn't going to go into her past right now. Maybe never if she didn't have to. But the Cult could still succeed if the priests didn't realize the danger and she might have to reveal her past to get them to stop the Cultists. "The Cult has only one goal and it's not the lies and half-truths they tell when they recruit."

"Are you satisfied, Brother Janks?" the High Priest asked. "Did she answer your question to your satisfaction?"

Janks gave the High Priest a sharp look, but nodded.

Do any of you have any more questions, Brothers?"

Only silence answered him.

The High Priest bowed his head for a moment, then raised it and opened his mouth to speak.

But before he could say anything, Janks spoke. "I abstain myself from both championship and the hunt."

Frowning, the High Priest looked at Janks.

"She has the regard of the Beast." Janks gestured to the sworlot who was glaring at the High Priest. "I will not go against such."

Muttering broke out amongst the priests again.

"She's an off-worlder!" an older priest yelled out. "Degar would not soil so!"

"I know what I have seen and what I have read in the scriptures." Janks paused to let that sink in a bit before speaking again.. "I have come to my own conclusions. What the rest of you do is on yourselves.”

There was more muttering, then movement amongst the priests. Several of the younger priests and a few of the older ones moved to stand behind Janks. One of the older priests stepped forward until he was beside Janks.

“Brother Baks,” The High Priest looked surprised to see him there.

“Your Highness.” Baks steepled his hands in front of his chest. “I request that we annul the judgement due to unusual circumstances and revoke the challenge.”

The High Priest frowned as more muttering swept through the priests around them.

“This is more than just off-worlder nonsense or interference,” Baks told him. “And should be discussed in an enclave with her as witness.”

Louder mutterings swept through the priests.

“There is no precedent for this.” The High Priest was still frowning with a troubled look. “Off-worlders are not allowed in an enclave, much less as witnesses.”

“Like Brother Janks I believe she has Degar’s blessing and we need to heed her words.” The priests behind him and Janks nodded as Baks spoke. “We have grown complacent and the off-worlders are taking advantage.”

Sara bit her tongue. Only the Cultists were taking advantage as the Federation as a whole let the local governments mainly alone. She would have to set them straight later. They needed to be consolidated. Or at least as consolidated as the priesthood could be with the type of people most of them were. Just had to find something that would motivate each to act the way they should to this threat.

"I will suspend the judgement and consider your words." The High Priest steepled his fingers before his chest, closing his eyes.

The Priests gathered in groups and muttered to each other while the High Priest meditated.

After a moment there was movement behind the High Priest. Sara saw a flash, but before she could say anything, the High Priest moved. He whirled, grabbed the knife out of the air, and threw it back, all in a smooth movement. The offending priest fell, the knife in his shoulder, and the High Priest glared as other priests rushed to the downed figure.

"Your Highness," Baks said.

With a last glare at the group surrounding the downed priest, the High Priest turned back toward Baks. "I knew someone would take the bait if I baited the trap just right."

"Your Highness?"

"Rolad could not have been working alone." The High Priest stepped forward and to the side so he was properly facing Sara. "I annul the judgement and revoke the challenge, Sister Lendri."

"You knew someone would attack you to put another High Priest in your place so they could execute me." Sara saw it all now. The High Priest wasn't reluctant because he didn't believe her or trust her, but was baiting the enemy within.

"I call an enclave."

"And this off-worlder?" Baks asked the High

Priest.

"She will be witness."

Baks bowed his head to the High Priest, then he and his followers swept out of the courtyard and into the temple, leaving Janks standing in front of Sara.

"You will escort Sister Lendri to the Chamber in an hour's time, Brother Janks," the High Priest told him.

"As you will, Your Highness." Janks bowed.

"I will leave you here with your companion, Sister Lendri. If he is to be with you you will be responsible for his behavior during the enclave."

"I understand, High Priest Nuet." She inclined her head to him.

He gave her a nod, then he too swept out of the rapidly emptying courtyard.

Sara waited until only she and Janks remained with Anwar in the courtyard before she turned her attention to the sworlot. He sat alertly at her side, his eyes on Janks.

HE HUNTED YOU.

"He did," she agreed, earning a look from Janks.

HE DOESN"T LIKE YOU

"I'm sure he doesn't. None of the priests probably do."

TRUTH

Janks looked back and forth between Sara and Anwar.

"I think he's realizing that what he said he believed may actually be true."

The sworlot chuffed, his version of a laugh if the amusement she was sensing was his because all she felt was the irony.

"He's not a tamed sworlot?" Janks asked. "Davad was a good tamer and I thought this sworlot might have been his. He's loyal to his friends."

"And you thought he would send his pet to defend me.'' She nodded. "He would have defended me himself if he had been still alive. Rolad killed him."

"What?!" Janks took a step back, overwhelmed with shock.

"Rolad had always been jealous of Davad. When his off-worlder masters ordered Davad's death, he did it gleefully."

"But…"

"A man who would betray his people wouldn't think twice about betraying his brother whom he was jealous of."

TRUTH

Sara went over to her pack and dropped to sit cross-legged on the ground. Pulling out the water bottle, she took a drink.

The sworlot followed her and lay down beside her with his head on her knee. She scratched behind his ears and he made a rumbling purr.

Janks stared at them for a moment, then spoke. "I'll be back to take you to the Chamber. No one should bother you here."

She raised an eyebrow but didn't say anything as he turned and left the courtyard. He no doubt needed time to come to terms with what she had revealed to him because she was sure the High Priest had meant him to stay with her until he was to take her to the Chamber.

TWELVE

The Chamber was deep in the temple. It resembled a theatre with seating on different levels facing a stage which had a podium in the center. Slim alcoves were in the wall behind the stage but Sara didn't see a use for them.

She followed Janks down the center aisle to the stage with Anwar at her heels. The seats were filling quite rapidly but she kept most of her attention on the High Priest who was standing at the podium. He was fingering a round metal object that carried a faint glow. As she walked up the stairs onto the stage, the High Priest threw the object at her and she automatically caught it, making it glow brighter.

Silence fell over the room as those who had seen it glow brighter stopped talking. The other priests looked towards the stage as they followed where the others stared and froze at the sight of the brightly glowing object in her hand.

Sara moved to the High Priest's side and stood next to him, facing the seats. Obviously the glow of this object meant something. "High Priest Nuet."

He held out his hand, and she set the object on his palm, making the glow dim. It disappeared into his robes as he turned to face the seated Priests, resting his hands on the sides of the podium.

"You're not going to tell me what that was about, are you?"

"Not yet." His fingers flexed on the podium and light seem to come from behind them. "I call this enclave to order."

Voices came from behind them, yelling something in the native tongue, and Sara turned slightly, her eyes widening in surprise. Each alcove was filled with a hologram of a priest. They were speaking the native tongue so she only got the gist of what they were saying. It seemed they didn't approve of her being here and were demanding answers.

The High Priest said something sharply in the native tongue and the hologram priests fell silent. "You are only here to receive my words so listen and do not speak," he told them in common tongue before turning back to the Priests in the seats. "We are in a troubled time. A group of off-worlders seek to lead us from our path. They have already subverted some of our brethren and people. I have set some trusted brothers on the hunt for those who would betray us and they have my permission to use lethal means.

"We have become complacent, making us ripe

for this insidious rot to take hold and flourish. The greed of sin has taken the place of our duties to both our god and the people, allowing the lies this group of off-worlders spew to corrupt us to the point of the betrayal of our belief.

"Degar has shown me the way through. Or rather he has shown me the person who will lead us through." He had to stop speaking as the priests were all shouting words at him in the native tongue. His whistle pierced the noise, and the room fell silent again as he raised his hands for silence. "Do you disagree with the signs, Brothers?"

"Your Highness." Baks stood from his seat. "I agree these are signs of favor. And I agree that this group of off-worlders mean us harm. The rooting out of traitors is justified. But I don't see beyond that."

"You think the off-worlders will stop?" the High Priest asked him. "After all they have risked and done?"

"Once the traitors are gone, they would have no toe hold. " Baks returned.

"There is no guarantee that we would get all the traitors or sympathizers." The High Priest paused. "And they only need to kill me to cause chaos among us."

Baks frowned.

"The factions among us," he reminded Baks. "Each would lobby for their own and tear us apart, keeping us from consolidating against them. Need I remind you of what happened in the courtyard?"

"She's an off-worlder." Baks looked at Sara. "How do we know this isn't part of their plan?"

"Would the Sphere light if it was?" the High Priests answered. "The group of off-worlders that guested with my brother came last month. Sister Lendri gave warning then but we did not heed."

"What about the Instruction?" Baks asked. "She doesn't know the Scriptures."

"She probably knows them better than you." The High Priest gave Sara a side look. "Do you not, Sister?"

"You knew I read your Book?" Sara asked with a raised eyebrow. That would explain a lot about things that had happen over the years.

The High Priest inclined his head.

"I have an almost photographic memory. " She looked at Baks. "Once I read something I can call it back up in my mind word for word."

"You know our holy tongue?" Baks frowned.

"Your written holy tongue is similar to the written language I grew up with. Didn't take me long to learn it." She paused. "However, your spoken tongue I'm still learning as it is not spoken like my native language."

Baks continued to frown.

"The off-worlders are correct in that Degar and Elgar come from the same source. A lot of the colonists that settled the outer planets came from the same place. Over time names and languages changed and thus the seemingly different Gods. The Death Cult of Elgar though burned their Scriptures and let Greed take complete control. They no longer care for their People…"

"We were beginning to go that path," the High Priest interrupted. "That is why they found supporters among us. We taught the Words, but did not follow."

I agree with that," Baks allowed. "But what you propose.."

Sara got a sinking feeling as she looked back and forth between them. She hoped her suspicion wasn't correct. "What are you proposing, High Priest Nuet?"

Before he could speak, a cry of rage and a knife came from the audience of priests. As Sara snatched the knife from the air, Anwar leaped from the stage into the audience, going after the thrower. Another knife was thrown before Anwar pulled down the thrower and Sara intercepted that one as well.

"They really don't like you, High Priest," Sara said. The two knives had been aimed at him. "Or at least whatever you're proposing."

Anwar dragged the priest to the stage by the neck, uncaring of any damage the rough travel caused. He laid the priest at Sara's feet, then moved back a bit, ready to act should the priest do anything but breathe and talk.

"What do you have to say for yourself, traitor?" Sara looked down at the priest.

A spat of the native tongue was her only answer.

Two priests climbed the stage, then dragged the other priest away with them.

"I gather they are going to question him?"

The High Priest nodded

"Are you sure about this?" Baks asked. "You could cause the very thing you hope to prevent by doing this."

"His attack reassures me that I'm doing the right

thing."

Baks steepled his figures at his chest and bowed his head. "Then I will support your decision."

"Thank you." He waited until Baks sat back down before speaking again. "Does any other brother or sister have qualms?"

The hologram priests shifted and muttered something in the native tongue, causing the High Priest to say something sharp, also in the native tongue, before he turned his full attention back to the seated priests.

"Your Highness." A priest older than Baks got to his feet.

"Brother Jame."

"The point Brother Baks brought up is valid. This may indeed cause a rift among us."

"You all saw the Sphere," the High Priest said. "Do you doubt its wisdom now?"

There were a lot of uncomfortable looks amongst the priests, but Brother Jame met the High Priest's eyes. "Not in of itself. She is obviously favored by Degar but what you propose... Such has not been for centuries."

"Perhaps that is why we strayed from the true path."

"Your Highness, may I speak?" A female priest stood at his nod. "Is it just that she's an off-worlder--or that she's female?"

More uncomfortable looks passed amongst the priest

The female priest glanced around, then nodded before sitting down. The looks had answered her question without any words spoken.

"I hope you are not proposing what I think you are, High Priest Nuet," Sara said. The look he gave her told her the answer. "I am no priest nor have I the desire to be."

"The Scriptures do not specify that the High Priest or Priestess have to be true priests, as you well know. Just 'favored' by Degar and instructed in the Scriptures."

Sara stared at him for a moment, then glanced at the surrounding priest before looking back at the High Priest. "There is a plan-ness about this."

"I had a vision when I first saw you at my nephew's side," he revealed. "Your face was lit by the glow of the Sphere."

"And the Challenge?"

"I would have done my duty," he said. "but mourned in private."

The sworlot stepped from Sara's side until he was nearer the High Priest who turned to face him. Anwar and the priest stared at each other for a moment, then the sworlot dipped his head.

TRUTH

So the High Priest was marginally on her side, but if she went against what he considered his duties he would follow them not her. "Why?" She knew the High Priest would know what she meant.

"You understand the enemy and know the tactics it will take to defeat them." He paused. "And I don't have the fortitude it will take to implement. I did not stick to my own plan for change. I allowed it to lie." He gave a smile at her look of surprise. "Where do you think Davad got his beliefs."

"It will take a lot of fortitude to defeat the Cult

and get back on the right path," she warned. "And much sacrifice."

"I believe my people have the strength to do it."

"But will they? Will they be able to fulfill the faith you have in them?"

"Once they realize what's truly at stake, I believe they will step up."

"So much faith." Sara glanced over the seated priests, pausing at Jame who still stood, before looking at the High Priest. "I hope it is well founded. Once started half measures will not do. They must be fully committed or the Cult will take advantage and could cause irreparable damage and harm to your people."

"So you will do it?" the High Priest asked. "You'll lead us along the Path?"

Sara stared out over the audience of priests. Some showed excitement, but most were apprehensive and a few were scowling.

CHOSEN

Her eyes dropped to the sworlot.

FATE IS WHAT YOU MAKE IT

With a nod, she chose her fate.

THIRTEEN

When the ex-High Priest motioned for her to take his place at the podium, Sara shook her head. "No, Father Nuet. You will be my assistant priest in this endeavor. I do not know the priests as you do."

"As you wish, your Highness." Father Nuet inclined his head to her. "What is our first order of this endeavor?"

"You have already started it; The rooting out of the Cult's supporters."

"Then?"

"More like simultaneous. Restrict the off-worlders to their Port. Any off-worlder found outside the base will be brought before me and judged. The Cult has been taken advantage of your Guesting-rights. All off-worlders with Guesting-rights will meet with me and will be judged. We need to route the Cult members out of the people as well as the supporters in the priesthood."

"This is preposterous!" One of the holographic priests blurted out.

Sara looked at the holographic priests. They were all scowling, but only the one had said something. "What did they promise you? Rolad was promised the High Priest position. Did they promise that to you as well?"

The priest sputtered.

"You disappoint me, Father Ren." Father Nuet frowned. "To believe their lies…"

With a flash the hologram disappeared. The other holographic priests looked shocked.

"Father Ren's temple is near the Port," Nuet told Sara.

"How much technology do you have?" There might be other reasons why the Cult chose this planet besides the obvious ones.

"Oh, everything our ancestors had plus what we've been working on since The Founding." Father Nuet's tone was matter of fact. "The Clans only wanted certain renewable tech but Our Founders kept everything."

"The Federation considers you a Level 3 civilization, barely above barbarians in social, and low in tech."

"That describes the Clans," Nuet told her. "That is how their ancestors wanted it but Our Founders knew that such would not sustain so the Priesthood was expanded. Somewhere along the Path we veered and thus we find ourselves in this mess."

"If the Cult has learned of your tech through

Father Ren or their supporters they would have no reserves about using your own tech against you."

"They would find that hard…" Nuet's words faded as a hologram flickered to life in the empty alcove.

An off-worlder in a spacer's coveralls appeared. His hair was shaved short and his eyes were a piercing emerald green while his face was like it was hued from a rock; all sharp features. He stared at Nuet for a moment, then turned his gaze to Sara. "I am High Priest Rance Tao. I am told you are now High Priestess."

Sara inclined her head but did not speak.

Father Nuet made a gesture and several of the priests got up and left, including Brother Janks. The rest of the priest kept their attention on the stage.

"As you can see, I have control of this temple and soon we will have the others," Tao said.

"Let me guess, you want us to just surrender and you won't harm any of us?" Sara's words were full of sarcasm.

"That is, I am sorry to say, not possible as you well know."

"You are not sorry at all."

"Death with no purpose is wasteful but re-education is not possible with some."

"You mean brain-washing." She paused. "Have you already started the Cleansing at that temple?"

A flash of surprise crossed his face before it went blank. "You seem pretty well informed about us."

"Let's just say my people were one of your failings."

Tao's eyes ran over her again, then widened

before the blank mask fell over his face again. "Ilan-decent."

"Ilan period."

"Not possible."

Sara gave him a smile that was more a baring of teeth than anything else.

"My followers should already have infiltrated your temple…"

Janks appeared at one of the doorways and nodded to Nuet.

"And my priests have taken care of them," Nuet interrupted. "I figured Ren had told you all our secrets, at least all that he knew. So I had my priests take care of it."

"Your priests? I thought she was the High Priestess."

She knew he was trying to drive a wedge between her and the priests but before she could say anything Nuet spoke again.

"She made me her assistant Father and as such they are my responsibility as well."

"Well, one of my brothers is even now gaining access to your system through this temple. Soon I will control your whole system network."

"I'm afraid not," Nuet said, moving a hand over the podium side. "As I was telling Her Highness, taking over the entire system from a single temple is impossible. Ren only told you his secrets. Now I think we've wasted enough time with you."

Tao's hologram flickered, then disappeared.

Sara raised an eyebrow at Nuet.

"I disconnected the temple from the grid, and shut down his power. He may get the generator to work at half power but he'll not be able to reconnect to the grid."

"You can do that to all the temples?"

Nuet inclined his head.

Two of the holographic priests disappeared, but the others gave Nuet a gesture.

"I gather he tried to take over the other temples as well and met resistance."

"As soon as Father Nuet gestured for a patrol we did too," one of the holographic priests said. "No one came to my temple."

The others agreed that none came to their temples.

"Father Hap and Father Pale are closer to the Port than the others," Nuet commented.

"Did the intruders have blasters, Brother Janks?" Sara asked the priest still hovering by the doorway.

"No. They carried stunners though."

"I gather you have some transporter of some sort," she asked Nuet.

"Yes."

"It would be risky but could some of you send priests to help at the other two temples?"

The other holographic priests looked at each other, then two froze. A moment later they unfroze and nodded. "I have sent a patrol to Hap's temple," one said while the other just said. "Pale's."

"Excellent. If we can confine him to that one temple with no hope of rescue…" She paused. "If they have communicators of some sort that would be even better. We can use them to talk to Tao and he'll know his followers failed."

Janks disappeared out the doorway.

"Is this his first move?" Baks asked as he stood.

"His first move was recruitment. This was his next move, but he had to speed it up because of me. He probably would have waited another month or even up to a year before taking over the temples. Whenever he thought he had enough supporters to get it done quickly and quietly. The Clans wouldn't have noticed anything right away not until Tao wanted them to. With your tech in his hands, he would have tighten his hold on the Clans and not worried about retaliation. And he was already sowing seeds of change. You don't think Father Nuet's nephews were the only ones they were talking with."

"Our straying from the true Path has cause discord amongst our people." Nuet paused. "We have much to repair."

Baks bowed his head and sat back down as Janks came down to the stage. He held up an oval object toward Sara who took it from him with a nod of thanks. While Janks returned to the doorway, Sara examined the object.

She had seen this before but hadn't expected to see it here. It was Cren. What would a Cren communicator be doing here. "This is from the intruders?"

Janks nodded.

"Were the stunners oval as well?"

Janks nodded again.

Cren weapons. "They're not just stunners."

Before she could say more, two holographic priests appeared in empty alcoves. They nodded to the other holograms, then looked toward Nuet and

Sara. "Secured," they both said.

"You should find one of these," Sara showed them the oval object. "on one of the intruders. Take it and the stunners with you when you leave. I do not care what you do with the intruders."

The two priests nodded and disappeared.

Sara looked at the other holographic priests. "Send a priest with the stunners and communicator here when they return."

"What is wrong?" Nuet asked.

"This is more than just a gambit for the Cult. It is the opening move for a Federation takeover by the Cren."

FOURTEEN

Silence followed her statement for a moment, then the priests muttered amongst themselves.

"How would this help them? The Federation…" Nuet shook his head.

"The Federation would either be involved in a civil war or divided up into different systems. Either way the Federation would be in turmoil and ripe for them to sweep in and take over."

"Why would they be in a civil war; they don't interfere in planetary governance."

"The Church." She paused. "The Cult will sometime try to take over a planet with a covenant or on a planet where the Church has a presence and another Ilan will happen. And this time the Government will get involved sooner. The Federation doesn't want another Ilan and they will step in, one way or another. But by then the Cult will have control of a lot of planets and have segregated them from the Federation."

"So, you believe the Cren are supporting this Cult to undermine the Federation."

"Probably not publicly even among themselves, but yes that's what I think."

"Should we prepare for them to step in when this Cult is defeated?"

Sara shook her head. "Not yet I think. I'm sure all of this is still secretive and the Cult is no doubt on a long timeline. I don't think the Cren will make any moves for at least a year and maybe not even then. Depends on what their agenda is specifically. Right now the Federation is strong but that may change due to other circumstances."

"You think this Cult may still go ahead with takeover plans for other planets?"

"I don't know. That's not my concern right now. This world is."

"What would you have us do?" Nuet asked simply.

"How does this transporter of yours work? Does it need full power on both ends?"

"No. But they won't be able to transport out with only half power and no main password if that is what you're worried about. As to the transporter itself it stretches between the temples' sending and receiving stations only."

"Excellent." She pressed the button on the oval object and it split in half, opening up with a flip. "Rance Tao."

"I am here." Tao's voice came from the communicator.

"We stopped the people you sent to the other temples." She paused to let that sink in for a second, then asked, "Do all your followers and priests know you're consorting with the Cren?"

"I don't know what you're talking about." His voice was carefully without inflection.

"The weapons and these communicators. Surely you don't think I'd assume you just happened upon them. Or not recognize them for what they are."

There was silence for a moment, then, "What do you mean? A supporter donated them for the cause."

"If you think I believe that you are telling the truth with that nonsense, I got a galaxy starship to sell ya,"

"You calling me a liar?"

"I'm calling you a traitor to humankind. Anything the Cren promised you is a lie. You ought to know whatever promise they make will be voided once they get what they want. After all you do the same thing."

"Such harsh words."

"But true." She paused as a priest entered the room with a small bag. He brought it straight to her and she motioned for him to sit it on the floor. She gave him a nod, then turned her attention back to the communicator. "As your supporters at that temple are now finding out. Is Ren even still alive? After all if he turned once he may turn against you."

"You do indeed know much about us." He paused as a voice spoke softly in his background. "Well, I have to go now, but we will be seeing each other again soon."

"Count on it," she agreed. The communicator closed up and she looked at Nuet. "I think he's got the power up. He'll be disappointed when he can't teleport out."

"What do you want us to do?" Nuet asked again.

"I'd like to pay him an in-person visit." She raised a hand when Nuet shook his head and opened his mouth. "But I know that's not possible right now."

"Not for you. But we can send a patrol of priests to capture him," Nuet told her.

"He might not be expecting that if he can't get the transporter to work for him." She frowned in thought. Tao wouldn't think the transporter would work for them if it didn't work for him. "Does Ren know much about the fail-safes of the transporter?"

"None of them did." Nuet gestured to the holographic priests. "It is in the last Instruction that the former High Priest gives the new." He pulled out a small book from his robe and laid it on the podium. "This has all the secrets a High Priest must know."

"Isn't that dangerous to keep all your secrets in a book that can be stolen?"

Nuet opened the book and tilted it toward her.

It was written in the original language that their native tongue came from. Terrans wouldn't recognize it, and those of the language's decent would have a hard time reading it as language drifted over the centuries. Unless they had a teaching machine or curriculum that taught it as her people had.

"Fathers are taught this sacred tongue. Some of

the brothers as well if they have the aptitude." Nuet closed the book and laid it back on the podium. "That you could learn to read the Scriptures said you had at least a grounding in our tongue."

"And the sacred tongue as well." She gestured to the book. "My people's tongue came from that language as well. Unfortunately so does the Death Cult's."

"As I feared." Nuet held out the book to her. "This is now yours."

She took it and it disappeared into her clothes before she turned her attention back to the situation at hand. "We need to lay siege to that temple. Tao must not be able to forward his plans any further."

"You inferred that he's killing priests that he can't control." He paused as he waited for her nod of agreement. "Then if we send a patrol or two in, we may have a chance of taking back the temple by grabbing Tao. They'll be busy with the slaughter and not thinking the transporter is working..."

"That might work if the entry team is quick and quiet. They'll have to take supplies in case they have to stay a while."

"Not a problem. So we have your permission?"

"Yes."

"Brother Janks, if you would." Janks disappeared from the doorway at the Father's words and Nuet sighed. "It is started."

"The battle had begun the second your planet was picked. The course set the moment the first Cult member landed. You just didn't know it."

"True. I just regret the necessity of what is to come if we can't contain this by capturing Tao and taking the temple back."

"The Cult will not win," she stated. "I will make sure of that."

CHOSEN.

She looked down at the sworlot who sat at her side.

WE. WE WILL.

"We are committed to that as well," came Nuet's words over Anwar's.

Sara blinked as emotions--and memories--swamped her. Her sister had sworn in just such a way, and she remembered what had happened after. She pushed away the memories, locked them back up, and got a hold of her emotions. They couldn't influence her decisions. This was not then, and Tao was not the same High Priest who had ruled that time and that Cult. Things have changed as had she.

Many of this Cult's followers were thugs, witness the ones that had hunted her. They were not the same caliber as the ones who had guested with Rolad and Davad's father. Those had been educated, though still fighters and so were no doubt priests. But the hunters had been thugs, pure and simple. This new Cult had much to offer them. Protection and power being the main draw for such, and money. Ill-gotten gains, no doubt.

The original Death Cult was much different. Their priests were educated and disciplined in different styles of fighting with a code of conduct. They had various sources of income that were legitimate as well as tithe from followers. The only thing that would be called bad was their sacrificing to what the Church considered a pagan god.

Which was the very thing that caused the strife between the Church and the Cult.

"Father Nuet." A priest appeared at the doorway. "Brother Janks has sent the completion signal."

"That was quick." Sara looked at Nuet. "Maybe too quick."

"A different signal would have been sent if they had been captured," the priest at the doorway said. "Brother Janks planned for that."

"Thank you, Brother." Nuet gave a nod to the priest, then looked back to Sara. "I suppose you want to go to the temple and confront Tao."

"That was my thought."

"I have another thought."

"I figured you did."

"Brother Janks can bring Tao here." He held up a hand to stop her words as she opened her mouth. "Tao will not escape. And even if he did he could do nothing damaging. Trust me on this. Please."

Sara stared at him. She only truly trusted one person, everyone else was a calculated risk.

CHOSEN

She looked at the sworlot.

TRUTH

"Alright." Her eyes went to Nuet. "Bring him here."

"Thank you." Nuet looked to the priest by the doorway. "Brother, send the retrieval code."

The priest nodded and left.

"I know you are leery of letting Tao near the center of our technology but he truly can't damage or take control of anything here. Ren gave him access, yes. But this temple is different in more ways than one. You will see."

Sincerity shone in his eyes, and Sara nodded. She would indeed see. As she planned to be there when Tao was brought here.

FIFTEEN

The transporter room was a big bay of space in the lowest part of the temple. In the center of the room was what looked like a giant Dyson sphere with a half circle control unit to its right. Standalone electric torches lit the area around the controls but the sphere itself was lit by laser grids. Sara had never seen a transporter like this before.

"Father Nuet."

"Something we created that was more--feasible," he said from beside her.

They were standing behind the two priests at the control unit with five other priests. Anwar was sitting beside the control unit with his eyes on the sphere. When she had express that she wanted to be here when Tao came, Nuet had had the five priest escort them both here. Now they were waiting for a signal from the other temple or rather from Janks.

"More feasible." She gave him a side look.

"Uses the same amount of energy but transports more with less accidents."

Before Sara could say anything one of the priests at the controls spoke. "Signal received."

"Then bring them home." Nuet turned his full attention back to the sphere.

"Aye." The priest ran his fingers over the controls.

The sphere began to rotate faster and faster until it was a blur, then there was a flash of white light and eight figures were suddenly in the center of the sphere. Slowly the sphere stopped spinning and Sara could see the people inside clearly.

Tao was in the center of the group wearing shackles but he seemed awfully calm for a man among enemies. Sara had smelled something fishy already, but this made her even more wary.

"Anwar." She looked at the sworlot.

The sworlot stood as Tao, Janks, and the others left the sphere. As soon as they were clear of the transporter, he stalked over to Tao, the priests moving out of his way, and stared at the suddenly twitching Tao. Tao tried to back away but the priests wouldn't let him move.

DECEPTION

"Did you search him thoroughly?" she asked Janks.

"Nothing on him."

"What about in him?" she returned. "He could have had something implanted."

Tao tensed but the priests grabbed his arms and

held him still as one of the tech priests stood with a device in his hand. He flinched when the device went off before the priest even reached him.

"A locator." The tech priest returned to his seat. "The shielding here is keeping it contained for now. But when you move him from here." He shrugged.

Nuet nodded, then looked at Janks. "The shielded cells."

Janks nodded and led his group and Tao out of the room.

"He thinks his followers will get him out somehow."

"Yeah, he's got a plan of some kind," she agreed. "You sure they won't be able to use the transporter?"

"We snatched them back so no."

She nodded, then looked at the sworlot. "What did you get from him?"

FEAR. DECEPTION. FEAR. RECOGNITION. SMUGNESS. DECEPTION.

"In that order?"

The sworlot dipped his head.

Sara pulled Nuet away from the other priests and turned to look at them. "Tao recognized one of your priests, Father Nuet."

Anwar stalked toward the priests but before he could reach any of them, the tech priest who had scanned Tao stood with a Cren weapon in his hand.

"Brother Bix," Nuet spoke in a disappointed voice. "I thought better of you."

"You're the only one then," the priest returned. "Brother Tine, join the others."

"Stay where you are, Brother Tine," Sara said.

Tine remained seated, his eyes on the still advancing sworlot.

Bix fired at Anwar. The sworlot growled but advanced another step. He fired again and Anwar took another step.

With a flick of her wrist, Sara threw a shirikan, causing Bix to drop to the floor in a spasm. Anwar had distracted him enough for her to act.

The other priests grabbed him and hauled him to his feet, keeping him upright. Nuet glared at him for a moment, then gestured for them to take him away. Two priests dragged Bix out of the room while Nuet turned to Sara.

"You knew it was him."

"Yes." The order of the impressions Anwar had got had told her that much. "Do you know how your investigators are coming with rooting out the Cult's supporters?"

"Brother Dal, if you would check on that for me?"

One of the other three priests nodded and left.

"Father Nuet. Your Highness." Janks appeared in the doorway. "Tao is settled in the cell. I left two priests there with him."

"Hopefully they're not supporters." Sara glanced at Nuet who frowned. "Shall we go see him now?"

With a bow, Nuet gestured for her to go first.

Janks turned and led the way with Sara and Nuet behind him and the two other priests following them. The sworlot lagged behind them all. They went up two floors and down a long corridor to a heavy wooden door with a barred window at the top.

"These are our special cells," Nuet told her as Janks opened the door.

"You said something about shielded." Sara stepped in behind Nuet.

The area held five small cells with iron bar doors. Each cell had a bunk, a composting toilet, a small sink, and a small table with a pitcher and bowl on it. Crude looking but Sara could make out the faint glow around the bars and hear the equally faint hum of a force-field. Tao was in the back cell with the two priests standing on either side of the cell watching him.

"I hope you're finding your accommodations comfortable, Tao." Sara moved to stand two feet from the cell, Anwar at her heels.

"That's High Priest Tao your Highness," he snapped at her.

"Not here." She shook her head with a little smile that could be mistaken for a smirk.

"Your little takeover is all but finished. We are hunting down your remaining supporters even as we speak."

"We will yet be victorious."

"Father Nuet." Brother Dal had returned from his mission and had joined them. "Brother Bix is spilling his guts to Brothers Ban and Til. They said that they should have this all cleared up within the hour as there doesn't seem to be many supporters in this temple."

"We are not close to the Port and do not have as much contact with the off-worlders as the other temples." Nuet turned his attention back to Tao. "As we said your supporters are being hunted. They won't have time or the inclination to rescue you or anything else you're thinking of."

"You're alone, Tao."

"But not defeated." Tao moved and sprawled on the bed. "You may get my supporters and many of my followers, ending the threat here, but the second you captured me my priests followed protocol."

"Leaving this planet as quickly and quietly as possible so there will be no trace of them if the Guard shows up." Sara nodded. "So the Federation will just put it down as a local rebellion, pirates, or some such."

"As I've said before you seemed well informed."

"You think we will turn you over to the Federation who would have to let you go as they would have nothing on you criminally." She moved a little closer to the bars. "Then you can go ahead with your takeover plans for the other planets."

"I don't know what you're talking about. I was just visiting a priest friend of mine when you all snatched me."

"You really should read all the rules and regulations on these rim planets."

"What do you mean?" Tao frowned at her.

"While we eventually do have to turn you over to the Federation, if you're alive, the regulations don't specify when or in what condition." Nuet was the one who answered him. "We are allowed to punish you for your part in the wrongdoing."

Tao straightened.

"The inner worlds have been a part of the Federation for a long time, but these rim planets have not. And there are more Federation Ports in the inner worlds than out here as you well know. So local justice is more widely used in the Rim." She paused. "However it is written in all planetary rules and regulations. The Federation doesn't like to stick its nose into everything; it can't and be effective. Not as a democracy anyway."

"So you will be our--guest for quite some time, Tao," Nuet said.

"You can't do this! You have to turn me over to the Guard on Port!"

"Eventually yes. But not for a while." Nuet gave him what was definitely a smirk. "Any plans you had will just have to be put on hold."

"Meanwhile rumors of your planned takeover will be spread. As well as the rumor of you consorting with the Cren. It won't be easy trying this again elsewhere once that is hinted at. The weapons and communicators are going straight to the Portmaster which means that rumor will be all over Port within a few hours."

Tao glared at her.

"I would not have another Ilan," she told him. "Or the Federation turned into a Cren breeding ground. Did you really think the Cren wouldn't take over all the planets? Humans are meat slaves. They would massacre your people just as much as they would the rest of the human race."

He continued to glare at her but kept silent.

"We wasted enough time here." She turned and headed for the door. "Brother Janks, he is your responsibility for now. I have a meeting with the Portmaster that I need to get set up. "

"As you wish, your Highness."

Sara, Nuet, and the three escorting priests swept out of the holding cells with Anwar at their heels.

SIXTEEN

Nuet led them back to the transporter room once they exited the holding cells. Two priests sat in front of the control unit again with two other priests standing behind them.

Father Nuet." Sara stopped just inside the door and looked at Nuet. "I'll need the bag with the Cren equipment."

"Brother Dal." Nuet nodded and gestured toward the door, causing Dal to leave. "I'm going with you as are these Brothers."

Sara opened her mouth to protest, but Nuet raised his hand to stop her words.

"While I trust my brothers with my life, yours is something different."

"That's why you haven't left my side." And why she had made him her assistant priest. She didn't trust anyone much less these priests.

He gave her a tilt of the head.

"You think the other Father and brothers could attack me when I transport to the other temple." She had calculated that risk as high but the Federation needed to be warned about the Cren.

Another tilt.

"Anwar would massacre them." Of that she had no doubt.

"Perhaps. If he had the chance."

"I'm not as easy to kill as you think." She paused. "Not as easy as my poor performance in the courtyard portrayed."

"I know." He held up a hand. "But I do not wish to tempt my priests just yet. Nor do I want to have to find a new Father from what would be left after you and the sworlot were done."

She stared at him. He seemed sincere.

Brother Dal returned just then with the bag.

"Is he coming too?" she asked in a sarcastic tone.

"Yes." His voice was firm.

"Then he can hold on to the bag for now." Her voice was resigned. "Which temple is closer to the Port; Father Hap's or Father Pale's?"

"Father Hap's. Two days travel High Port side."

"Excellent. No risk running into any of Tao's followers still on planet. They'd all be Low Port."

"You sure? What about his 'priests'?"

"Two days from now? They'll all be off-planet. Rats deserting a sinking ship. Rich rats, but rats none the less. Just like his followers. The Priests would have just left, telling only a few what was happening. They would just leave the rest to the mercy of the Guard or your priests. Followers are replaceable, priests are not. Supporters even more so."

"That is just wrong. Followers are the heart of a religion."

"Not to the Death Cult. Followers mean different things to each of your religions. Have you ever played the Terran game chess?"

"We call it Mocar." Nuet said. "We priests play it quite regularly. Some of the Clan leaders know it as well."

"To the Death Cult followers are pawns, to be sacrificed for a play. Supporters are interchangeable with pawns or rooks depending on the play and his priests are knights and bishops with the High Priest being both king and queen. Those who aren't members of the Cult are the other player's pawns. And the High Priest plays with them all as if it were just a game of chess."

"People are not chess pieces." Nuet frowned.

"No, they are not," she agreed. "But that is how Tao looks at the world. How the whole Cult is trained and raised to look at the world. Other people are pawns, worth nothing but what they can do for you."

Nuet continued to frown at her. "That was where we were headed. Some priests already think that way."

"Yes." She would let him stew on that for a bit. They had other things to do right now. "How do we get this thing going?" She gestured to the sphere.

"Right." He shook his head. "Brother Tan."

One of the tech priests ran a hand over the control panel, and the sphere rotated until there was space to enter it. Nuet led the small group with the sworlot following inside to the disc set in the center of the sphere. Once everyone was on the disc it rose a few feet up, and the sphere began to rotate around them.

Sara could feel the energy build as it picked up speed and, anticipating the result, she closed her eyes. Goosebumps raised her skin, then a flicker of electricity swept across her body. Her eyes flashed open, and she could see the sphere around them was visibly slowing down. Further out she could see they were in a different, but near identical transporter room.

Three priests stood beside the sphere holding drawn bows with two more priests behind them. Nobody moved as Nuet just stared at them

After a moment Anwar glided out of the sphere and glared at the priests, causing the bows to drop to him. He rumbled and continued to glare.

Nuet stepped out of the sphere first, the others just behind him. "Such an aggressive greeting, Father Hap."

"Can't be too careful," said the older of the two priests behind the bowmen priests. He had his priests lower their weapons which they did though they kept wary eyes on the sworlot. "How may we be of service?"

"We need five small travel packs and a guide to the Port."

"As you wish. Brother Mani," he said to the priest next to him. "If you would."

The priest nodded and left while Father Hap turned his attention back to Nuet. He seemed to be ignoring Sara but she knew he was well aware of her. The tension in his body told her that much. Father Hap was not happy about the state of affairs with her as High Priestess. But then she didn't expect any of the older priests to be. Or some of the younger ones. She was bringing change. No sane person liked change though most know it was inevitable and needed.

Father Nuet frowned at Father Hap. Sara knew he was angry at the disrespect being shown but she had other things on her mind than disapproving priests. She could correct their attitudes later.

Anwar glided over to her and lightly leaned against her legs, rumbling a purr.

She laid a hand on Anwar's head and scratched behind his ears, causing the purr to get louder. The priests gave Anwar wary but awed looks, though Hap kept his face neutral. Sara could tell by his eyes that he was impressed even though he didn't want to be.

Brother Mani returned with five full-looking shoulder bags hanging from his arms and one slung over his own shoulder. He handed them to Brother Dal who then passed them around to the rest of the group.

Sara accepted hers but adjusted the strap and slung it cross ways. If she had to move suddenly she didn't want to lose it. The others readjusted as well so they too could sling theirs cross ways, and Nuet merely shrugged when she looked at him.

"I gather you'll be our guide," Nuet said to Mani.

"Yes. I know the short route to the Port the best."

She kept her thoughts on that bit of statement to

herself. After all it could be just her paranoia speaking. She was going to give the benefit of the doubt but keep her eyes open. Like she was with Nuet. Trust no one, ally or enemy. Humans are treacherous beings for all their capacity for tremendous compassion.

Nuet gestured for Mani to lead the way and he fell in to step behind him. Sara followed Nuet with Anwar at her side and Nuet's three priests brought up the rear. They took the quickest way through the temple to the front doors, and Mani took them to a trail that started to the left of the gate where he paused.

"It's used enough to make a trail but it is not as smooth as a route," Mani warned them before stepping on the trail. "Be careful with your steps," he added over his shoulder as he continued walking, leading them on.

SEVENTEEN

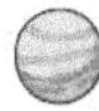

The group made the Port by Dawn of the second day. Taking the short way took hours off and they had only napped for a few hours during the previous afternoon. Nuet had kept them moving with short rests only when necessary. They had barely spoken during the trip. It was if they all had sensed an urgency. Sara knew why she was in a hurry to get to the Port, but she was unsure about Nuet's motivations.

High Port's gate loomed ahead.

Federation Ports were made up of three sections, each with a gate that led out of the force-field and stone wall that surrounded the entire Port. High Port was quality businesses, Rich people's domain while Low Port held civilians, military and lower businesses and the third part was for the local businesses, local government offices. In the center of the Port was the landing grid for ships. The Federation had had a time clearing this land and keeping it clear while they built the Port. Even now the force-field was more for keeping the jungle/forest back, then any security feature.

They halted before the metal Gate. It had a ten foot frame but the shimmering metal doors were only eight feet high. The doors inlay was engraved ivy. A Terran joke no doubt, but it made the Gate fancy looking instead of plain. To the right of the door was the intercom on a stand also engraved with ivy. Since this Gate faced the jungle/forest it was probably less used than the two other Gates that opened into the local Clan's community. Though the Priests seem to use this Gate.

Brother Mani went to the intercom and pushed the buzzer.

"Yes?" a male voice asked.

"We're here to see the Portmaster."

"Do you have an appointment?"

"No, but it's important enough for the boss to be here," Mani answered.

The Gate buzzed and the doors swung open a little. Mani led the way in. Anwar however refused to enter.

I WILL WAIT.

Sara nodded and entered with the others.

Inside was a small metal airlock like chamber. It was just big enough for the six of them to enter and have the doors behind them close. Sara could feel the scan the chamber ran over them but the expected warning about what was in the bag Dal carried never came. So now she knew how the off-worlders had gotten blasters past the Guard. Someone had reprogrammed the Gate sensor. She looked at Nuet who raised an eyebrow. So he knew too then. But she shook her head to tell him to let it lie right now.

With a hiss the sealed door at the other end opened to reveal a Guard in his blue and tan uniform. "The Portmaster awaits you. Please follow me."

They fell into step behind the Guard as he turned and led them down the street. To the right were various buildings that were obviously businesses while to the left was the stone wall and force-field that surrounded the Port. Other streets branched off here and there to the right as they continued. Ahead and to the right was a three story steel and glass building with the Federation logo on its front. That was where they were headed.

Another Guard was standing at attention by the glass front door. When they approached he pressed his hand on the scanner by the door and it slid open. Both Guards nodded to each other, then the group was led inside.

Plants and water dominated the lobby. There was a fountain between the two elevator banks and flora with little ponds were randomly set about the room. A door was discreetly set on the back wall next to the left elevator bank. Sara knew that led to a Guard post.

The Guard led them to the right elevator and once they were in he pressed the top button. Doors closed and the elevator moved upwards. It opened seconds later in an outer office. Two people in Port

Green coveralls waited by the receptionist desk and the Guard stopped in front of them.

"Mr. Cran and Ms. Chan," the Guard greeted them. "Here are the Guests."

"Thank you, Officer." Ms. Chan said. She watched him move back to the elevator and go into parade rest before turning her attention to the group. "I am the Assistant Portmaster. Portmaster Yog is waiting for you in her office."

"Brother Dal, you will come with us, you two stay here," Nuet told the others. "If you will, Ms. Chan."

Chan inclined her head and led them through the half-open door behind the desk.

An older woman sat behind a fancy wooden desk in an equally fancy chair. Two wing-back chairs were in front of the desk and a fancy console was set up behind the woman, but the rest of the office was empty. No pictures or file cabinets. Just wooden walls. Sara was surprised that there was no sign of her high status. Even her clothes were the Port Green coveralls that all Port employees wore, though hers had a red patch on her left arm.

"High Priest Nuet, this is rare," the Portmaster said. "Usually I have to meet you at the Clan House."

"This is too important to delay. First, I am no longer High Priest," he paused as he gestured to Sara. "This is Lendri, our new High Priestess. You need to listen to what she has to say."

"Does this have to do with the exodus of people and the large amount of violent crimes that has been happening the past two days?"

"Yes."

"Honesty. How refreshing." Her smoky voice was wry. "Please sit."

Chan left the open door and moved to stand behind the desk next to her boss while Nuet and Sara slid into the wing-back chairs with Dal standing between them. Sara hid a smile when she glanced at the open door. She knew the receptionist was listening and that the Portmaster wanted him to but for a different reason than she.

"That exodus was priests of the Death Cult." Sara said the words matter of factly.

"The Death Cult was destroyed when their High Priest was assassinated seventy-some years ago." The Portmaster stated.

"That's the propaganda that the Federation circulated, but they merely went underground. Building up their resources until they could begin their campaign with what they believed a near one hundred percent chance of winning."

Yog frowned at Sara but before she could say anything Nuet spoke. "They exist, Portmaster. We have their High Priest in a cell in the main temple."

The frown deepened as the Portmaster looked at Nuet.

"He tried to take over my temples. He will face justice." His voice and words were firm.

Her eyebrow raised.

"As I was saying the exodus was the priests. But the violent crimes increase is from the followers that they left behind. They recruited the scum, the displaced, the disaffected, promising them whatever they desired as well as no doubt getting them hooked on Chini, making them obedient in order to get their next fix. With the priests leaving the followers digressed, turned on each other, and went back to their previous behaviors. As the withdrawal gets worse some of them will become sick, others will die, and a few will shrug the drug off though they will have problems with their senses. Chini is nasty business.

"As to the attempted takeover. We have taken care of that. Tao will be punished accordingly." Sara paused and gestured for the bag. "But we came here for another reason." She stood up, took the bag, and upended it on Yog's desk. "The takeover teams were carrying these."

Shock was on both women's faces as they stared at the Cren equipment on the desk.

"H-how?" Yog stuttered.

"Your scanner at the High Port Gate has been recalibrated. I'd check them all if I were you just to be sure it's the only one. Because I don't believe it is. As to how the Cult got them, I think they made a deal with the Cren."

Denial was written on both of the women's faces this time. The Cren had overrun a rim planet a century ago and the horrors and savagery the Federation revealed when they took the planet back had made humankind's blood run cold. So much so that Humans declared the Cren persona non grata in Federation ruled space. Any Cren ship spotted received a lethal response by the Guard, and every new planet that joined was shown the aftermath of the overrun planet. No human in their right mind would go within ten feet of a Cren, much less make a deal with them.

"The Death Cult doesn't view human life as valuable. Except their own of course. But others?" Sara shook her head. "I'm sure the Cren told them sweet lies about how the Cult would rule the planets and the Cren would just co-exist with them. Seventy-two years ago the Cult was on its way to ruling half the known universe, then Ilan happened. Their own followers saw how they were viewed expendable by the priests and acted accordingly. Only the diehard priests and followers remained, and the Federation had declared them outlaw. The Cult wants to rule again, and they will do it anyway they can, even make deals with the devil. Though I think the High Priest made the deal without telling his priests. Or just his closest confidant."

Yog and Chan stared at her.

"It is now in your hands." Sara stepped back from the desk. "We have reported the attempted takeover, and delivered the forbidden weapons to you. What you do with them and the information we've given you is up to you. The Cult may try a takeover elsewhere but it failed here. Losing their High Priest is only a temporary holdup for them. The next ambitious priest is already vying for the position no doubt if Tao's confidant hasn't taken over himself. So they will not be slowed for long."

"This failure will not dissuade them?" Chan asked.

"No." Sara shook her head. "One planet is nothing when half the galaxy is at stake. This will set them back but they will forge ahead."

"I will make note of your report to the Guard,"

Yog said. "and turn over these weapons to them After that it is up to them to follow up on anything off planet. The scanners will be looked into and more patrols will be scheduled for Low Port. That I will see to."

"Good enough." Sara tilted her head to Yog. "Thanks for meeting with us, Portmaster."

Yog tilted her head to Sara.

Nuet stood and the three of them left the office.

"I will guide you back to the Gate," the Guard said as he straightened from the wall beside the elevator door.

"I want to go to the temple in the Clan's community," Sara said to Nuet. "It should be cleared by now."

He looked at her for a long moment, then nodded to the Guard, "If you would take us to the LoCom Gate."

The Guard bowed and pressed the elevator button. Once the elevator opened, he gestured them inside before slipping in just before the doors closed.

EIGHTEEN

It took them two hours to get to the LoCom or Local Community Gate. It was next door metaphorically speaking to the High Port Gate but not literally. Traversing the many streets that separated it from High Port took time. The suns were well on their way to midday and the heat was oppressive, though cooler than the jungle/forest as the force-field filtered the rays.

Once at the Gate, the Guard left them and they went through.

They came out on the beginning of a street in what the Federation would call a small town. Wood and stone buildings dotted the giant clearing with the large temple at the end of the street. Clan communities held the businesses and schools of the Clan as well as some Guest housing so they were a town of sorts. A lot of the actual work took place at

Clan homes but offices were held in the Clan communities as well as some of the actual work. It depended on what work that particular family did. Clan members were not always of the same family. Clans were made up of different families, though the Chief had to be of the original Clan family.

"Brother Dal, if you would be so kind as to run ahead and acquaint them with our arrival," Nuet said as they paused just outside the Gate.

With a nod, Dal took off at a trot toward the temple.

Nuet turned toward Sara but before he could say anything, Anwar joined them from the encroaching jungle/forest. He stared at the sworlot for a second, then shook his head before returning his attention to Sara. "I assume you have a reason for wanting to visit this temple so soon. I won't ask but I feel I should warn you that you need to be on your guard. My presence should retard most unsavory actions but…"

"I understand." She gave a nod. "And if I find what I think I will you'll know why as well. Depends on if it was destroyed when Tao was captured and before they evacuated. He wouldn't have wanted it too far away."

His eyebrow went up but true to his word Nuet didn't ask what she meant. He simply turned and led them towards the temple at a fast walk. Even though it was daylight a few Clans members moved about them and Nuet nodded to those who nodded to him but he didn't stop walking.

The temple gate was closed as was wont during daylight hours, but Nuet gave a whistle and they slowly opened to reveal the courtyard and the front of the temple. Two priests waited there with Dal.

All temples were built to resemble the main temple though without the many underground levels. Two basements were all the land-based temples had and Sara thought to find what she hunted in the lowest, near the transporter and generator. But she also had other business she had to attend to.

The priests bowed to Nuet and her.

"We need to go to your lowest level near the generator." Sara got straight to the point. She could take care of the other business on the way there.

With another bow, the priests led them in through the sanctuary and out the door behind the statue into the corridor. Taking a right they followed the corridor to the stairs and went down two flights.

Just as they stepped off the stair, Sara held up her hand. "Stop. I'll just be a moment," she said before disappearing behind the door marked "Necessity".

Necessities had crude composting toilets. A congruity in their tech.

Sara indeed only took a moment and rejoined the group but laughed when Nuet took this time to disappear behind the door as well.

Nuet rejoined them and they continued toward the generator with Sara eyeing the markings on the few doors along the corridor.

At one of the doors she stopped them. "We will look in here first. If I do not find it then we may have to do a systematic search. He would love the irony of putting it here."

Nuet entered with her but stayed by the door as she stepped further into the room. Two bulky machines lined the side walls and a control console sat between them. Sara moved to the console as she figured he would have set it up there. When she rounded the console she saw what she had come for.

The device was set on the chair. It was oval with a squared off base like an giant egg sitting in a box. The box part had several buttons and a small screen was built into the oval part. Sara moved to it and squatted beside the chair.

"What is that?" Nuet had moved to the console and was staring at the device.

"A bomb. Of sorts, anyway." She ran her hands over the oval part. "It's not primed thank goodness. Tao probably thought he still had a chance so he didn't arm it. Not to mention he wanted to live a long time."

"I don't understand."

"The wave this device gives off acts like an EMP pulse to machinery but is like radiation to humans." She carefully laid the device on its side so she could pull off its bottom and reached in and removed a glowing green stone. After laying the stone on the console, she then put the bottom back on and righted the device. "One of the priests should take this to the Port."

Nuet went to the door and called one of the local priests in.

"Here." Sara handed the priest the device. "Take this to the Gate and tell them it's compliments of the High Priestess."

With a nod of his head the priest left.

Sara picked up the hand-sized stone and stared at it for a moment.

BAD STONE

Anwar had been quiet and she almost forgot he was there so it startled her a bit when he projected his thoughts to her.

"Very." She agreed.

Nuet cleared his throat.

"You probably wonder how I knew to look for this."

"Crossed my mind."

"The Cren don't like losing. If they were routed they would do one of two things. Had they time they would evacuate and raze the whole planet from orbit. If not they would set off as many of these bombs as possible, destroying technology and irradiating the people. I figured the Cren would send along one in case this insurgent failed. Tao probably wasn't the only one who knew about this but the other probably didn't want to die either."

"It would have knocked out all electronics?"

"Everything that needed energy to run. This close to the Port, well they would have been affected too, though the force-field would have weakened the force."

"You think there was only one?"

"I don't know."

Nuet opened the door and spoke in a low tone to the priests out in the corridor before closing the door and turning back to her. "They'll institute a search for anything alien."

"I hope you told them not to touch it."

"I did."

Sara nodded, then dropped the stone to the floor and stomped on it. She continued to stomp on it until it lay in dull pieces. The priests would want to study it and it would be a temptation for the Federation as well. No human had gotten an active stone before, during or after the War. The Cren's whole power system ran on those stones but the Cren destroyed everything if there was even a hint of them losing. But the Laren had known and had planned accordingly. Thus ones like her.

She had a feeling the Cren had only sent the one device. One might be chance, but if more were found, conspiracy. So she was not worried that they would find another bomb, but other things, maybe.

"What did you mean about irony?"

"The Cren name for this bomb sounds similar to the word 'trash'. So waste disposal…"

"Ah."

"Can we transport back from here to the main temple? I have some questions for Tao."

"Of course." Nuet opened the door and gestured her through. "I too have questions."

Sara looked at him but his face gave nothing away. She was sure the questions was more for her than for Tao.

NINETEEN

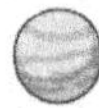

An hour saw them back at the main temple and at the holding cells. Tao was sitting on the bunk and glaring at them. When they had first come in he had tried ignoring them, but Anwar just sat at the door staring intently at him, and Tao had transferred his glare to them from the wall within moments.

Sara smiled at him, just to irritate him. His glare hardened which made her laugh at him. He was so easy.

"You will pay for this!" he yelled at her.

"No, you will," she told him. "Your erstwhile allies have abandoned you and your priests have deserted you as per protocol. You will take the fall and 'pay' for this. The only chance for leniency is if you answer our questions truthfully."

"You're going to kill me anyway. Why should I

tell you anything?”

“If you don’t tell us voluntarily then torture it is.”

“You wouldn’t. Federation law…”

“As you well know planetary governance disputes are handled locally. That is why you choose this planet, isn’t it?” Sara reminded him. “The natives can do what they want with you.”

“You’re not a native; You’re a Federation citizen.

“Actually I’m not.”

Nuet looked at her.

He had seen her ID that she had used since coming here, but it was fake. It had been made for her so she could travel without questions. If she needed to.

“What?”

“Ilan never had the chance to join the Federation.”

Both Tao and Nuet stared at her.

“You can’t be Ilan,” Tao said. “It’s just impossible. We hunted down and wiped out those that survived the genocide.”

Nuet looked at Tao, frowning.

“A survivor killed the Prophet…”

“Cori Nino was no prophet,” she told Tao. “ Just a power-hungry man. Like you.”

“How…How do you know the Prophet’s true name?”

“The Ilan that killed him.” She paused and met Tao’s eyes. “That was me.”

Tao was shaking his head.

“How…” Nuet gestured at her.

"Magic," she told him, looking at him. "Perhaps you might want to rethink this High Priestess thing. I'm going to live a long life."

"Better to keep us on the Path then." Nuet's words were firm.

"You lie." Tao moved toward the barred door. "All the Ilan are dead."

"At least two are not." Sara slid closer to the door, Anwar at her heels. "The Death Cult follows Elgar, yet you despise his people. Without Elgar's Ilan you wouldn't exist as you are."

"You lie!" Tao lunged against the barred door, and screamed in pain as the force-field repelled him. "You lie," he repeated in a hoarse whisper.

"Not about that."

Tao slid to the ground and started to mutter to himself.

Sara stared at him for a moment, then turned to Nuet. "It won't take much to get him to talk now."

Nuet also looked at Tao before returning his attention to Sara. "So I think as well...Are you alright?"

She gave him a faint smile that held little humor or happiness. "As I'll ever be."

"Let us retire to my--your new quarters." He turned toward the door. "We have things to discuss."

With one last glance at Tao, she followed Nuet with Anwar at her heels.

They ascended the staircase to the ground floor and took the main corridor until they came to double carved doors. Brother Dal opened the doors as the two other priests stood guard on either side.

Nuet and Sara with Anwar entered and Brother Dal closed the doors behind them, standing by the door as Nuet led her deeper inside.

The room they entered was obviously the receiving chamber with two couches facing a wing backed chair. Nuet led her through the antechamber behind the receiving room into the personal chambers. An archway to the left led into what Sara could see was a bedroom while an archway to the right led to an office. The room they were in was a living room with a small four chair dining table and two couches set around a fireplace in the back wall. It was cozy and there was an air of warmth to it. Sara liked it.

Nuet led her into the office.

A large carved wood desk dominated the room. Scrolls and papers covered the desk and books occupied the wooden bookshelves on the other three walls. Two wing backed chairs faced the desk and Nuet settled in one of them.

Sara settled in the other as Anwar lay on the floor next to her chair.

Nuet and Sara stared at each other silently for a moment, then Nuet sighed.

"I know you have no reason to trust me or the priesthood but at least listen to what I have to say and give me--us--the benefit of the doubt." He paused and waited for her nod before continuing. "When you first came, my brother and I thought you were either a government spy or a Church missionary but Davad said not and persuaded his father to Guest you. That is when I had that vision. I decided to spend more time at the family home though it put my brother out a bit."

"I had wondered."

"Davad sang your praises to me whenever he could, and you didn't sing any praises at all. I decided to test you."

"That's when you brought your Book."

"Yes."

"I guess I passed, seeing as you made me High Priestess."

"When you objected to the off-worlders, I believed you. But my brother did not; he believed the lies they told. And now both his sons are dead."

"He's going to blame me for that, not his own poor decision."

"Yes." He stopped speaking and looked away.

"I can see you have more to tell me."

"The off-worlders. I should have kicked them off-planet or at least restricted them to the Port. But I didn't want to go against Guesting rights just on your word or my uneasiness of off-worlders."

"You couldn't know what they were planning. I didn't know, just that they were bad news. Like that first wave of Church missionaries on Ilan. Da said they were agreeable and friendly while sowing the seeds of discontent about Elgar's religion behind the Priests' back. Besides Rolad stood by them."

"Yes, Rolad. Who I knew was angry with me and the Priesthood for not being considered adequate."

"I knew he hated the family business, though he was slotted to take over."

"Because he was rejected by the Priesthood. If he had been accepted then it would all have fallen to

Davad."

"He hardly talked about his own family. He talked about the Clans, even his own, but hardly anything substantial about his father or brother, just you. Anything I learned about Rolad I observed, same with his father."

"Davad was more like me, to his father's dismay. My brother is a serious man, little sense of humor, whereas I can be serious but I see humor in life."

"Like the old saying that life is too important to take seriously?"

"Exactly." A brief smile touched his face before he became serious again. "When I became High Priest I was tired. Tired of greed, of the hypocrisy. Like many of us who fully read the Book during our time as apostles I had ideals but after six months as a Priest I was beaten down and just went along with the status quo. I thought when I became High Priest I could change everything. But I was more tightly bound. I have changed some things but I fear that when I die things will get worse."

"Thus me as High Priestess. You can change something and blame me, and keep your beloved status."

"Partly. But I do believe you can lead us into a better future."

She stared at him for a while before speaking. "I still haven't forgiven you for the Challenge debacle, but, as this crisis has shown, we can work together. Your priests have a lot of change ahead of them, and they'll not like it. Are you prepared for the backlash?"

"Are you?" he returned. "You're the one they

will resent the most. Assassination attempts will probably be a daily thing, poisonings though maybe not every meal, and disobedience."

"That's what you're for." She gave him a smile before becoming serious again. "The poisonings are non-issues. I throw-up anything that can harm me. As to the assassination attempts, I can defend myself. My poor performance at the Challenge notwithstanding. And as I said, the disobedience that is what you are for."

"Brother Baks has lobbied for some changes. He may support us, at least nominally."

"Politics are your area, Father."

Nuet nodded.

"Now I have a question for you." She paused, waiting for his gesture to continue. "Do you have a long range communication device? Something that can reach into space, I mean."

"Our founders did have something similar to a Para-beam like the Port has, but unfortunately that technology got lost through the centuries. However, we do have a sub-space relay, well a station of one anyway."

"Where is it? And is it in working order?"

"Here." Nuet seemed amused. "And yes."

"Here?" Sara glanced around, not seeing another doorway. "Or do you mean in the temple?"

Nuet stood and moved to the bookcase on the right. After he pulled our a book, there was a grinding noise and the shelf divided, swinging open a little.

Sara jumped out of the chair and joined him, peering into the opening.

The room was the size of the office with two walls covered in electronics. A control console sat near the center of the area with a monitor sitting in its center while the rest of the room was taken up by a bulky old-fashion generator. It had obviously been built back when the colony had been created.

"It was set down by our founding fathers that we keep this operational." He opened the door wider then led her inside. "They didn't explain why, but they were quite clear."

There had been one on Ilan in the old city capital. She and others had been trained in the use and the destruction of communication devices, both before and after the *Bran*. The priests and the Laren wanted their warriors to be able to communicate to them and to stop the enemy from communicating.

Nuet started the generator then moved to the console as the generator rumbled to life. He flipped a few switches, then stepped back and gestured for her to take his place.

Sara stepped up to the console and typed a quick message. It held a warning and a brief summary of what had happen. Anyone with sensitive equipment would register the message but as she had written it in Ilan, only one other would be able to read it. She glanced over it one last time then hit the send button. It would take a while for her sister to get the message but she would at least be warned and she would know what to do.

A beep sounded, telling her that the message was sent, and Nuet stepped up. At her nod, he turned off the console then moved to shut down the generator. "I believe we have more things to discuss," he told

her as he gestured to the door.
    She nodded and led the way out.

TWENTY

Once they were both back in the office and sitting in the chairs, Nuet began. "You mentioned restricting off-worlders to the Port. But the Portmaster said there was an exodus. Do you still want to do that?"

"For now. We can allow off-worlders back on a case by case basis after a while."

"Including the Professor's party at Strader?"

"Them most of all." She wanted the investigation into the cave and chamber at least slowed if not stopped. Humans were not meant to know what may be hidden in that cliff.

SPY THERE. NOT HUMAN.

Sara had figured there was a spy amongst the Professor's group. No way Tao wouldn't put one there just in case. But if Anwar said the spy wasn't human, then maybe the Cren had the spy. Or maybe two spies. Either way they needed to leave.

"I shall set the wheels in motion tomorrow for their extraction and send out a message to the Clans revoking Guest-rights to off-worlders for the time being. There's not that many outside the O'don Clan."

"The Clan near the Port?"

He nodded then asked, "And after the off-worlders are back in Port? What then?"

"First your priests keep hunting the Cult's supporters. No way are they all found yet. And not just in this temple. Rolad probably spoke to many other priests."

"And through me he had that access." Nuet nodded again, sadness and regret radiating from him.

"You are not to blame for his actions, Father Nuet. If anyone beside Rolad himself should take any blame it would be Tao or the Death Cult itself. They provided the temptation."

"If the Priesthood had accepted him…"

"He would have still spread poison. And had more time to do it. I think he was bad from the start. The level of maliciousness he contained--it had to be there from childhood. He was envious of Davad. This I know. It festered, then the lies Tao no doubt spewed just took him over. You are not to blame."

"I knew there was discontent between them. My brother thought it was just brotherly competition, but I knew better."

"You are still not to blame. Do I need to keep repeating that until you get it through your thick skull?"

"Maybe." Nuet sighed. "I just keep thinking there should have been something I could have done that wouldn't have ended with both my nephews dead."

"This is how it was to be. Tao set this course in motion when he came here. Elgar or Degar, whichever God you believe, brought about our meetings. If He hadn't wanted this outcome, it wouldn't have happened this way."

Nuet bowed his head.

"Now while your priests hunt down the supporters we steer your priesthood back on the Path laid out in the Scriptures. With a little moderation."

"Might need more than a little." He laughed. Determination was in his eyes, though, as he looked at her.

"Which is where you and your politics come in. While I have a long time yet, you do not, and others may not agree to continue where you leave off. So we need to get a lot done before it is your time."

"You will still strive, won't you, even then?"

"As long as I can," she told him. "But I can't promise more than that. Your priests need to want to change to keep it going."

"Hopefully by my time most will see the rightness."

"Straying has more visible rewards."

"Unfortunately true." He sighed. "But I-we-must try. I fear another takeover, but internal this time, and that would be disastrous for our people."

"I must warn you that your founding fathers weren't all that altruistic. Better than what you have now but they still upset the Clan-rule thing that your ancestors were going for."

"I suspected as much from the research I did as an apostle. But the Highland Clans were heading toward a civil war with the Lowland Clans. And the Highland Clans had the advantage with the basket."

"That's neither here or there." She made a dismissive gesture. "I just wanted to warn you that your founding fathers weren't perfect and neither are their Scriptures. The moderation I was talking about has to do with that. Some of the rules are too rigid and some are too liberal. They will have to be modified to fit this society better."

"As long as they are not too changed, I can live with that."

"But can your priests?"

"I'm sure there will be trouble. I can promise you that. But I will support you as long as the changes are for the betterment of the priesthood and the Clans."

"A warning in return." Which it was. He was telling her that as long as he agreed the changes were necessary and right he would follow her lead. No blind trust. "Just promise to argue with me in private and not in front of your priests. Request a private audience if you must should we be in company."

"I agree." He paused. "This is historically the High Priest's chambers."

"Are there other chambers nearby?" she asked him. "I'd prefer smaller chambers."

"The Temple Father's chambers are just before these. They are smaller. Just an office/receiving room and a bedroom."

"Perfect."

"I'll have a brother pick up your things from my brother's house."

"If he hasn't destroyed them."

"If he has then we will just get you more from the Clans or the Port." He straightened in the chair. "Perhaps you should get some sleep. We can discuss more tonight."

"Only if you promise to at least get a nap in as well. Tonight begins the first step into a new beginning for your priests. Humble beginnings."

Nuet winced.

"Don't worry I won't make them wear sack-cloth or anything like that or give up all their privileges. But living better than the Clan Chiefs is over for your Fathers. And Tithing needs to be evened out, no more extra demands. Passing the plate is one thing but demanding extra Tithing is another. Your priests need to learn to live frugally and within their means."

Nuet winced again.

"They can do it but it will be hard." Sara stood and patted him on the shoulder. "I know you'll be the one they complain to but you are the one who appointed me High Priestess. So you really brought this upon yourself. Now show me to my room."

Giving a sigh, Nuet stood and moved toward the door, Sara following with Anwar at her heels. He led her out into the corridor and down a few feet to an arched door.

Dal and the other priests were gone. Off to their own sleep no doubt.

"This is the Temple Father's rooms. I will leave you here." He turned back to toward the High Priest rooms. "I will be back at eight bells to take you to the dining hall."

"Can you see about something for Anwar?" she asked as she opened her door. The sworlot went inside as soon as the door was wide enough for him to slip through while she talked to Nuet.

"I'll talk to the cook. Good sleep."

"You as well, Father." She stepped into the room, allowing the door to close behind her.

An archway to the left led to a bedroom that she suspected had a privy but the room she was in was a combination office/receiving room. It showed recent habitation but she was not worried she was taking someone's bed. Nuet would have said something.

The sworlot rumbled from the bedroom.

She flipped the lock on the door. Hopefully she would not be disturbed by intruders.

SLEEP.

"You're right." She turned away from the door and headed into the bedroom. Not even pausing to undress, she flopped onto the bed and went limp. It felt good to be on a bed. The sleep she had gotten on the cot in the Professor's camp hadn't been restful and the catnaps she had the last three days had been more tiring than being awake.

SLEEP

The word held impatience.

"This has almost been anticlimax after all the anxiety I had. I never thought I'd live past the challenge. Rolad was more skilled than I."

I HATE DISCUSSIONS.

"What?"

Weight next to her told her that the sworlot had jumped onto the bed beside her. She turned her head and stared at Anwar.

SKILL IS NOT ALWAYS A DECIDING FACTOR. LUCK PLAYS A PART. ALSO IN THIS CASE AN OUTSIDE FACTOR. ME. NOW GO TO SLEEP.

The sworlot collapsed on the bed and closed his eyes. As she continued to stare at him, he scooted closer until he was against her and began a soft raspy purr.

Her eyes went close involuntarily and she relaxed into the mattress. She started to drift but hovered on the edge of sleep. It was hard for her to give up that last bit of awareness. Everything still didn't seem real and she was afraid that if she surrendered to sleep she would never wake up. That this was all a hallucination brought on by dying.

Intensifying his purr, the sworlot gave a huff of exasperation.

SLEEP

The word pulled her down to a dreamless sleep. A place where she was safe from everything, even her own thoughts.

EPILOGUE

Greenpeace
1321 Standard

Sara laid a hand on the stone coffin as the others left the burial chamber. Though Nuet had not technically been High Priest she had him laid to rest in the burial chamber anyway. He had been her right hand in this crusade and deserved it more than she.

Anwar leaned against her legs in support. He had a little gray mixed in with his fur now, but he was still as active as he had been when they first met. The Laren had enhanced his lifespan as well when they had messed with his genetics.

Caer had died decades ago. But she had never gotten another Hawk. He had been a gift from Davad and it hadn't seemed right. Besides she hadn't had much time for hunting after she became High Priestess.

Nuet had outlived their enemies, so too his friends. But he had lived long enough to see his dream come true. The priesthood was back on the Path the original fathers had set forth. With a few minor changes to go with the times.

It hadn't been smooth sailing at all. Within a few years, a War broke out between the Cren and the Federation. Greenpeace joined in when the Cren tried to take over the Rim worlds and with other Rim planets help to turn the tides. But many died and the priesthood was nearly decimated. Sara and Nuet had had to build it up from scratch nearly which in a way was good as the new priests were taught right the first time. There were a few holdouts of the old ways but they died out and new priests took their places.

"Should I take my leave now, my friend?" she asked the coffin. "Neo can run the priesthood and I can fade back into the trees. Anwar and I can be free again."

YOU PROMISED TO CARRY ON IF HE DIED

"That was long ago. At the beginning." She looked down at the sworlot. "The goal has been reached. Don't you want to roam? Be released from responsibility?"

WE CAN TAKE A REST IF YOU"RE TIRED, CHOSEN

The sworlot had gotten more talkative over the years but not overly. He still hated to converse yet spoke when he needed to. To talk sense into Sara mainly.

"It's more than being tired." Her eyes returned to the coffin." He was why I kept going. It was his vision. But now he's gone."

"Father Nuet said you might leave once he was gone." A young priest stepped up to her. "He made me promise you would not leave alone if you did not stay."

"I'm never alone. Anwar is with me."

"You know he did not mean that, Sara."

"Sara, huh? Must be serious to call me by my name."

"I am."

"Neo--"

"No, for once you will listen to me. Father Nuet didn't fear anymore for your physical safety. As you say Anwar is always with you. But your mental health is another matter. He feared you would spiral into depression when he died and do something rash. I agree with Anwar that you need a rest, to get away for a while. My father would welcome you at his house."

"I need freedom. I would spend some time in The Eade."

"Ana and Anon have expressed dissatisfaction with their training again."

"Our problem children. You want me to take them along with an eye toward assessment or to get them out of your hair for a while?"

Neo didn't say anything, his face neutral.

Sara stared at him for a moment. He didn't want to lie to her so he said nothing which meant another reason. One she wouldn't like. Babysitters, then. "I don't need watching over."

"You shouldn't be alone. And Anwar doesn't count. Not for this."

TRUTH

"You too?" She looked down at the sworlot.

THOSE TWO DON"T RESPOND TO THIS TEACHING.

"To the priesthood, you mean."

The two apostles spent more time in the jungle/forest than the temple. And while they were intelligent they didn't take to book learning. If you showed them how to do something they got it right away and remembered anything they were told. But sitting around reading and writing made them restless and they barely passed their tests. They were both orphans and their Clan had sent them to the priesthood to relieve some of the financial burden they were. So turning them away wasn't an option.

"Wasn't your Clan-friend a tamer?" Neo asked, his face still neutral.

"You want me to teach them to be tamers?" She could. Davad had passed on his knowledge on to her and she had helped him with his work. But she hadn't done the work for over fifty years, though her memory was still as good as ever.

"They can't stay apostles forever. They have to be able to contribute to the Clan or they will be outcast. The Clans don't suffer freeloaders as you know."

"Unless they're Clan Chief or his children," she retorted angrily. She'd had a hard time getting the Clan Chiefs to keep orphans past fifteen. Children were precious to the Clans but if the child didn't have family, the Clan threw them out of the Clan past the age of fifteen if they failed to find another Clansman or an apprenticeship to take responsibility for them. Nuet and she had changed that way of thinking for the most part after the war. The Clans couldn't afford to lose any more of its people so some changes were implemented, but the Clans still saw them as burdens and retained the right to outcast them if they were a financial drain.

"They would be a boon to the Clan," he told her.

She knew he didn't want to discuss her opinions about certain Clan Chiefs and was bringing her back on track. "Have you even talked to them about this possibility?"

"Yes," was his surprising answer. "Just before I came back here."

"Well?" she asked when he didn't continue.

"They were speechless with excitement of the chance."

"Or fearful." Of many things including of her.

"It was excitement I saw. Once I got them to believe it was possible, that is."

"You're serious." She looked at him.

He nodded.

When Davad had died his method of taming had died with him as he'd had no apprentices. Sara was the only one who still knew his method and thus the only one who could teach it. But for all that she was the High Priestess, she was still an off-worlder.

"Would the Guilds accept them? I am after all an off-worlder."

"They would accept it as Davad's Legacy. The

teacher doesn't matter."

If the Guilds accept it as a Legacy, then he was right. The teacher didn't matter. Most Legacies were taught from a book or journal by a family member of the one who's Legacy it was. It kept things from getting lost when someone died unexpectedly without a fully-trained apprentice or journeyman. Davad hadn't left behind a journal but had her. His legacy had been in hiatus while she helped fulfill Nuet's dream but now she could pass on what Davad had taught her.

Neo must have seen her answer in her face because he clapped his hands together with visible glee. This was a win for him as well. He got rid of two problem children and would be fulfilling his promise to Nuet.

"Tomorrow night when the gate opens," she told him. "Have them ready."

"You will have to have an enclave. This will be longer than your 'vacations'."

"Set it up for later tonight."

"Moons' zenith." He nodded. "I will take good care of the responsibility you have set me."

"You have during my vacations so I expect the same now, though it will be longer." She looked at the coffin. "I want to be alone now."

He bowed to her, then turned and left the Chamber.

"You have planned this out as well, old friend," she told the coffin. "I see your hand guiding Neo in this. You talked with him and contrived a new mission for me. A mission you know I wouldn't say no to."

The sworlot huffed.

She gave a sad smile. True, she rarely said no to Nuet's suggestions. He had been the one who knew people the best after all. So this really shouldn't have surprised her.

Bells pealed through the temple signifying the tenth hour. She needed to show herself at the Wake above before the enclave. The celebration of the end of an era you could say. Tomorrow night would be the first step into a new era.

With one last caress, she turned from the coffin and headed toward the door, Anwar at her side. She had lived two full lives filled with conflict. Perhaps this new--and probably her last--one would be kinder.

ABOUT THE AUTHOR

This is T. L.'s seventh book but the first in her Time-Lost Series. Each book in this series introduces a strong heroine who changes the course of the future. The books lead up to a final reveal that launches another series - The Sacrim. These Time-lost books are written in a different style than her other books in a completely different universe. So be aware if you decide to try the other books.

The blog for this series is http://www.time-lostseries.blogspot.com

She lives in Southern Missouri with a bevy of feral cats.